The Captain's Men

Preface

One of the greatest thefts of all time occurred in the year 1204 when the great city of Constantinople, the capitol of the Byzantine Empire and the seat of the Patriarch of the Orthodox Church, was under siege and in the process of falling to the crusaders of the fourth crusade. That was when the captain of a company of English archers and his men made off with two of the Church's gold-covered right hands of Saint John the Baptist which baptized Jesus, the silver-covered head of Saint Paul, and various other priceless relics.

The archers carried the relics to their company's base at Cornwall's Restormel Castle, and put out the story in the taverns and alehouses of Rome and various seaports that the Orthodox priests charged with rescuing the relics had hidden them somewhere along the Greek coast. As a result, the coast was constantly searched without finding them and the relics remained undisturbed in Cornwall until the archers attempted to sell them some years later. That was when the trouble began.

Chapter One

The world in chaos.

The world was a dangerous place in the spring of 1213. It was everywhere in chaos and turmoil. As a result, it was relatively easy for the Church and its churchmen to earn coins by selling prayers for peace and requiring donations of land in exchange for promises of salvation and less time in purgatory after a someone died.

England was still in turmoil even though it had been some years since King Richard had foolishly fallen to a boy's crossbow bolt and had been replaced as king by his landless and sole surviving brother, Prince John. John had taken the throne after Richard's death and promptly alienated many of England's barons—by immediately levying taxes to pay for his wars to regain the lands in Normandy that Richard had lost to the French. He also distressed the barons with his efforts to make and enforce laws equally throughout England instead of letting each baron make his own, and by prohibiting the barons from collecting tolls on the roads and paths across their lands.

King John refused to back off from the changes he had ordered. As a result, the barons were unhappy with him in 1213 and things looked to be getting worse instead of better—and once again there were rumours of war between John and England's unhappy barons and several of the more ambitious of them were thinking seriously of going after the English throne and so was Prince Louis, the heir of King Phillip of France.

Similarly in turmoil was Constantinople, until recently the most important city in the world and the former capital of the great Byzantine Empire. The city had fallen a few years earlier to the crusaders who had defied the Pope and attacked it instead of continuing on to the Holy Land to fight the Saracens and free Jerusalem. The winners were now fighting amongst themselves for control of the once-great empire's lands and revenues.

Perhaps best of all, if you look at it from the point of view the Cornwall-based Company of English Archers whose heavily-armed transports and galleys could earn more coins whenever there were refugees willing to pay dearly to be carried to safety, the Islamic armies were making gains throughout the Holy Land and the Moors in Tunis and Algiers were fighting a war of conquest in

Spain and paying for it by capturing and selling Christian slaves and ships.

There was no doubt about it, the civilized world was in chaos and upheaval, and a brutal and dangerous place to live and die—and therefore an absolutely splendid place for a company of English archers to earn their coins by using their war galleys and transports to carry refugees and cargos to safety and selling their services as mercenaries.

Some bright spots existed despite the brutality and lawlessness of the times. The Templar knights, for instance, were continuing to acquire coins and land by letting people touch the point of the spear that killed Jesus and pray near it—and then becoming even richer by becoming moneylenders and loaning out their coins at high rates of interest. They did so whilst trying to live as much as possible like Jesus which meant staying away from women and never washing themselves nor wiping their arses since Jesus, being a God, did not have to do so.

The chaos and fighting was similarly enriching the survivors of a company of once-penniless English archers who had gone crusading with King Richard and been left to die when Richard suddenly went home without them. The archers had somehow acquired two old war galleys from a poxed sea captain so they could escape from the

Saracens and return to England—and then discovered that they could earn coins for themselves by using them to carry pilgrims and refugees to and from the ports of the Holy Land.

Capturing Moorish prizes and using their initial galleys and their prizes to carry passengers and cargos to and from the Holy Land and other ports turned out to be so profitable for the company and its surviving archers that William, the one-time ploughboy who had risen to become their captain and led them as they fought their way home, had been able to settle the archers in Cornwall where they had first landed when they returned to England.

Much more importantly, the coins and prizes earned by their transports and war galleys enabled William and the surviving archers to recruit and train replacements to refill their company's ranks and expand their fleet of galleys and cogs. They also enabled the company to equip its new recruits with the latest and most modern weapons such as longbows and bladed pikes and take the time necessary to fully train them in their use.

As a result of being able to replace the archers who had fallen, and despite his several rather serious wounds, William had been leading his ever-increasing number of archers and galleys back to the Holy Land each year to earn even more coins and expand his fleet by taking Moorish prizes and by carrying passengers and cargo. He even permanently stationed some of the archers in galleys and shipping posts serving London and various port cities around the Mediterranean.

Things were also going quite well in poverty-stricken Cornwall where William had set up a training camp for the archers' new recruits. Soon after their arrival the archers had killed the murderous Earl of Cornwall and William took his place by buying the earldom from the king; similarly, his priestly brother became the bishop of Cornwall's diocese of few priests and many monks by buying it from the Pope.

Everything was all done fair and square according to the traditions of the time. The price of each of the titles was cheap because Cornwall had little value to anyone except the archers who needed a place to train their new recruits and did not want to be bothered by interfering lords and greedy priests.

The conflict between King John and his barons was good for William and the archers. And so were John's wars with the King of France regarding the ownership of Normandy. They were good because they distracted King John and the barons from paying attention to the growing strength and fighting abilities of the archers whose main quarters and training camp were located far away in Cornwall—and whose relatively small numbers and circumstances had led William and his sergeants to adopt new ways of fighting and train their men to use most modern of weapons such as longbows and long-handled bladed pikes.

Neither King John nor his military leader, Sir William Marshall, understood the archers or how their harsh experiences had taught them to fight and earn coins. Neither, for that matter, did England's nobles, such as the Earl of Devon who wanted Cornwall for himself.

Their ignorance was understandable. None of the archers were knights or attended court, and Cornwall, except for its tin mines which already belonged to the king, was well known to be so poor that even the Romans did not bother to build a road to it. It was little wonder that Cornwall and its archers were unknown and ignored by almost everyone of any consequence in England, and greatly feared and respected everywhere else where people knew them.

The conflict and chaos, and particularly the fall of Constantinople, provided great opportunities for both the archers and for people outside of England such as the Pope in Rome. The Pope, for example, saw the fall of Constantinople, where the papacy's great rival, the Patriarch of the Orthodox Church, had been located for almost a thousand years, as an opportunity to acquire more believers for his church and thus more coins and power for himself.

The Orthodox Patriarch and many of his bishops had abandoned Constantinople and its priests and parishioners to their fates and had fled on galleys hired from the English archers as soon as it looked as if the crusaders' attack would be successful. Indeed, they abandoned their flocks of believers and sailed away so quickly in order to save themselves that they also left behind the Orthodox Church's priceless relics such as the two gold-covered right hands of Saint John the Baptist and the silver-covered head of Saint Paul.

At first, the Patriarch and his bishops thought the relics had been lost and probably destroyed when Constantinople fell and was sacked. They had, however, charged a couple of priests with bringing the relics to safety, and were overjoyed when the rumour reached them that the priests had escaped with the relics and hidden them somewhere along the Greek coast.

The rumour turned out to be true—the English archers confirmed that their galleys had carried the priests and relics to safety and landed them at several places on the Greek coast. Unfortunately, according to the archers, none of them had gone ashore with the priests and they did not know where the relics had been hidden. Now the priests could not be found and no one knew the whereabouts of the priceless relics.

In Rome, Pope Innocent had heard about the missing relics and desperately wanted them. The Holy Father wanted them because it was well known that God answered the prayers of believers who prayed in the presence of the relics and made donations to the church in their name. The Pope believed that having the relics in Rome would cause some of the Orthodox believers to switch their prayers and donations to Rome, and away from the Orthodox Patriarch who had been forced to flee from Constantinople and settle in Nicea.

There were no flies on Pope Innocent III. He knew an opportunity when he saw it—he promptly offered the total avoidance of purgatory and great papal recognitions and indulgences to any prince or king who would find or buy the missing religious relics, and donate them to Rome. The Patriarch responded by making similar offers.

The Pope and the Patriarch were both wrong—the priests charged with saving the relics had fled in the wrong direction and been massacred by the crusaders when the fighting intensified around the Patriarch's palace. It was William, the captain of the archers, and his men who had fought their way into the Patriarch's palace and carried the priceless relics to safety.

For some years the missing relics had been safely and secretly gathering dust in Cornwall's Restormel Castle along with most of the gold and coins from the Byzantine treasury, the gold and coins that the son of one of the earlier Byzantine emperors had promised to give to the crusaders if they would restore his father to the throne.

And it was all about to change—William and the archers had made an "arrangement" with young Pope Innocent through the Pope's teacher and mentor, Cardinal Bertoli.

If it worked, it would truly be a deal made in heaven for everyone involved: the archers would get a king's ransom in gold and coins in exchange for the relics, the Pope would get the relics without having to pay for them, and a handful princes and kings would avoid purgatory and get the Pope's blessing for their claims and ambitions—*if* they acquired the relics "from whomever finds them" and donated them to the church.

The archers' problem, of course, was that the princes and kings would also be able to donate the relics to the Pope and receive the many benefits on offer from the Holy Father if they seized the relics from the archers by force instead of paying for them.

Chapter Two

Once Again in England.

I was standing on the roof of the forward castle of Phillip's two-tiered war galley lost in thought as we entered the Fowey estuary and the archers pulling on the galleys oars began rowing us towards the mouth of the river. Henry and Peter stood next to me.

My two lieutenants and I had spent the entire voyage since we left Tunis pondering as to how we might safely turn the religious relics we recently announced we had "found" on the Greek coast into coins, lots of coins, since everyone including the Pope said they were worth a king's ransom.

For better or worse, we had reached an agreement with the Pope and the first part of our plan to sell the relics was underway. So far, so good. But how were we going to keep the relics safe until we could sell them now that everyone knew we had them? It was a question that perplexed us.

From the very beginning, our fear had been that King John or one of Europe's other princes or kings would try to seize the relics from us by force instead of paying us for them. That was why we had kept their whereabouts a secret until we could make an arrangement with the Pope, and why we had brought so many of our company's fighting men back to England to help defend them. And, of course, it was also why we pretended not to know where the relics were located and did not conduct a "search" of the Greek coast to find them until we had finalized our agreement with the Pope.

It was a good agreement and well-designed to increase the number of coins the relics would fetch for us when we sold them—less, of course, ten percent to Cardinal Bertoli for getting the Pope to agree to our plan, and twenty percent for Pope Innocent III himself. The Holy Father, according to Cardinal Bertoli, desperately needed the money because his family was still trying to pay back the forty mule-loads of silver they borrowed to buy the Papacy for him.

Basically, the plan which the Pope approved involved our selling the relics to a Christian king or prince who would then donate them to Rome in return for avoiding purgatory and obtaining the Pope's recognition of their claims to various additional lands and titles.

It was a winning plan for everyone—unless, of course, one of the princes or kings, someone like King John, for instance, tried to seize the relics without paying for them in order to donate them to the Church and obtain the benefits promised by the Pope. The possibility of our having to fight to keep the relics until we could turn them into coins had always worried me. It was why we kept their whereabouts a secret and they had been gathering dust in Cornwall where my men and I lived with our women and children when we were in England.

In any event, and for better or worse, our plan to sell the relics was underway with the agreement of the Pope—who, being a Church official, would almost certainly accept them from anyone even if we were not paid. That was why worries about our being set upon and robbed of the relics, instead of being paid for them, had been almost constantly on my mind ever since we finished raiding Algiers and Tunis and set our course for England.

But then, without my even realizing they were leaving, my worries about the safety of the relics drifted out from behind my eyes as we rowed passed Fowey Village and entered the mouth of the River Fowey that runs up to my home at Restormel Castle. They were replaced with a rapidly growing sense of warmth and excitement as I realized that in an hour or two I would once again be with my family—and a rapidly growing sense of anxiety and sadness because I would soon be trying to explain the senseless death of Anne in Lisbon six months earlier.

As we rowed slowly up the clear and placid river, I could only hope and pray that Anne's two sisters and our children were spared from being poxed whilst I was gone, and would be alive and well to hear my sad tale of her death in Lisbon. And, of course, I hoped the same for my oldest son, George, now grown to manhood and an archer. And also for my brother, Thomas, and his students who were being learnt to scribe and sum so they could help the Company's captains who, to a man, could not. *It also gave the boys a way to earn their daily bread as priests if they were not up to serving in the Company.*

"Well, done is done as the Good Book somewhere says; I will know soon enough if they made it through another year."

"It has been a while, has it not?" suggested Henry quietly with a wistful sound in his voice. "I surely have missed all the trees and green grass, and that is a fact."

"Me too, Henry, me too. It is good to be home."

******

A number of the galleys from our raid on Tunis were already tied up along the riverbank as Phillip's oarsmen slowly rowed us around the final bend in the river and we moved towards the floating wharf tied to the riverbank in front of the archers' camp where we put the learning on our new recruits. The trees and fields along the river were thick and green and there was a sense of a coming rain in the air from the clouds forming to the south. In the distance, once we got around the bend in the river, I could see Restormel Castle.

It was very impressive and, without even knowing I did, I gave a big sigh of relief when I saw it.

"Hoy Captain, and welcome home," shouted the grizzled whitebeard who caught the mooring line one of Phillip's sailors threw to him as our galley approached the wharf. He had the two stripes of a chosen man sewn on to the front and back of his hooded tunic.

I knew the man. *What is his name?* He was one of Harold's sailor men recruited during those hectic early days when we first acquired galleys and went to sea to earn our coins. From out of nowhere his name popped into my mouth from behind my eyes.

"Hoy yourself, Josh," I said as I jumped down on the dock and extended my right hand and clapped him on the shoulder with my left most happily. "It is good to see you again and in such good health. And how is your dear wife?"

"Tolerable well, Captain, tolerable well, thankee. Jane will be pleased that you asked."

Men and women were streaming towards us and a crowd began to gather even before we finished mooring and I jumped down on to the floating wharf and felt it move under my feet. Many of the men were wearing long, light brown Egyptian tunics like mine and Josh's. The only difference being that my tunic had more stripes running across its front and back because I was the company's captain.

The men and women in the rapidly growing crowd were a cheerful lot, no doubt because of all the prizes we had recently taken off the Moors and the prize monies that would soon be paid as a result. They did not know I had made a great mistake in not ordering Algiers to be sacked when we surprised the heathen and I had the chance. They also did not know that my plan to destroy Tunis had failed and cost me one of my dearest and oldest friends.

It was a happy arrival and my lieutenants and I immediately plunged into the crowd and began shaking hands, patting backs, and exchanging congratulations with our men who had managed to stay alive until we made it safely back to England. All the while we watched intently as Phillip's men began to unload the empty wooden crates that everyone thinks contain the missing relics.

* * * * * *

Things were just beginning to settle down when the crowd parted and my oldest son, George, my priestly older brother, Thomas, and one of my women, Helen, arrived all out of breath and red-faced from hurrying down the path from the castle. *Where is Tori?* Tori was not with them.

Thomas saw the worried look on my face as he led my family through the crowd with a big welcoming smile on his face.

"Do not worry yourself," Thomas said as we happily grabbed each other's arms and danced around. "Tori is fine and most pleased that you returned. She is up at the castle with your new daughter. The dear little thing is still recovering from the same sweating pox that carried off poor Anne's daughter last year at about this time."

A few seconds later, a laughing and crying Helen, the older sister of Tori and Anne, was in my arms hugging me and I had my arm around my son, George, all at the same time. *My God, George is a grown man and even bigger than me.* Out of the corner of my eye I could see Peter beaming as his wife showed him a little infant who had obviously been recently birthed, and the empty crates that supposedly contained the newly-found relics coming off Phillip's galley and. *Well, the crates were not totally empty—we had packed them with rocks so they would seem to be full if anyone tried to pick them up.*

We all walked together up the path to Restormel and I spent an enjoyable afternoon catching up on the domestic matters of my family and being told about what had happened and not happened whilst I was away. The big family news was that I had gotten Tori pregnant again during my last visit home and George's young wife, Beth, recently birthed an adorable daughter so that I am now a grandfather. She was handed to me to admire and promptly pissed on me as soon as I picked her up.

The big company-related news, according to Thomas and George who proudly and excitedly told me all about it as soon as we could talk privately, was that while we were gone both of the German princes vying for the Pope's approval to be the Holy Roman Emperor had sent clerical emissaries all the way to us here in Cornwall to reaffirm their interest in buying the relics for the Church "if they are found."

Both parties of emissaries arrived, just as the Pope had suggested they should, to tell us that they were truly interested in acquiring the relics and donating them to the Church. They even brought some useless gifts to prove their seriousness and good intentions.

More importantly, the princes' emissaries also brought substantial pouches of coins to help pay the costs associated with finding the missing relics. *And, according to Thomas, each of them looked around to gauge his prince's ability to take them by force if we found the relics and then refused to sell them to their prince.*

Similar messages and pouches of coins had come in by way of parchments delivered by couriers from the king of the Swedes who wanted the Pope's blessing to add the lands of the Finns to his realm, and from Phillip of France who wanted the Pope to bless his claim to Normandy and once and forever end England's claim to own Normandy's lands and titles.

Unfortunately no word had yet been received from the others who had been asked if they were interesting in buying the relics if they were found—the Doge of Venice, the two ambitious kings of the Latin Empire who were thought to have coins, and the Orthodox Patriarch. *Ah well, it is still early days.*

Similarly, no word of any kind had been received from King John of our own dear England. That was not too much of a surprise since he was so well known to be poor that the Pope had not even bothered to send him a parchment suggesting that he help pay for the search and gather up the necessary coins to buy the relics for the Church "if the English archers find them."

There also had not yet been any messages come in from the crusader lords who want the Pope to recognize and bless them as the rightful princes and kings over the cities and lands they took off the Byzantines when they captured Constantinople.

What had come in before I arrived, however, was a tough-looking courier from David Levi, the king's moneylender in London who had become my friend. *Probably because we were both common-birthed outsiders fighting to get ourselves and our families and men ahead in a world whose lords and princes did not want us to rise.*

David's courier was a big burly fellow carrying a battle axe. He and his two heavily armed personal guards had come in on a trading cog from London last week and had been patiently waiting for my return. They were waiting because I had scribed and couriered an inquiry to David when we had reached Lisbon.

The axe-carrier had brought a sealed parchment with David's response. I broke the seal and read the parchment carefully, and then read it again even more carefully. David obviously understood what I wanted and what he proposed was quite acceptable. I told the courier as much.

"I agree with Master Levi's proposal and the price," I told David's courier as Thomas nodded his approval. Then I used a sharpened goose feather to stir some water into a bowl of ground charcoal from the hearth and signed it.

"Please tell him I said his terms are acceptable and that it would be most greatly appreciated if he would proceed as soon as possible."

******

We had a hastily organized homecoming supper of sorts that evening and all of the company's lieutenants and four-stripe and five-stripe sergeants came to sup with me and my family. We were joined, as was always the case, by the inevitable band of castle cats which prowled under the table for scraps to supplement their usual meals of the castle's mice and rats.

There were a surprising number of them, sergeants that is. The benches along the long wooden table that ran almost the entire length of Restormel's great hall were packed even though Raymond was in Okehampton with our horse archers and Harold and many of our company's sergeants were in Cyprus assisting Yoram in his efforts to put some of our recent Moorish prizes into service carrying passengers and cargos.

As you might imagine, everyone cheered and banged their drinking bowls on the table when I stood up on my bench before supper started and confirmed that the valuable relics we had been seeking were now safely upstairs in the sleeping room above the great hall where we were sitting—and got even louder when I added that every man in the company would be getting prize money as soon as they were sold. *As you might imagine, I did not mention that they had been up there for some years.*

I also told my men what they already knew—that I had brought thirteen full galley companies of veteran archers with me, well over a thousand men, to help guard the relics. Then we settled down to drink and eat and tell each other stories and lies as old soldiers always do when they eat and drink together.

What everyone knew so thoroughly that my sergeants and I did not even discuss, was that the archers I had brought with me would be joining the more than one hundred and seventy horse-riding archers and outriders under Raymond's command at Okehampton, and fifty or so archers from our Trematon, Bossiney, and Launceston garrisons.

We also had the hundred or more veterans who were in the camp to school our newly recruited apprentice archers who were being learnt to push arrows out of a longbow, use the bladed pikes the Company's smiths have been making on Cyprus, and march together putting down the same foot to the beat of a rowing drum.

Furthermore, many of the four hundred or so apprentice archers now in camp had completed their training and were ready to put an archer's stripe on their tunic gowns and join the company. In addition, we had hundreds of construction and farm workers from among the local lads who were available to carry water and arrow bales.

There was no doubt about it, we assured each other; we had a powerful army of well-equipped fighting men available to guard the relics.

******

Supper was a festive occasion and Tori and Helen and all my children, even the youngest infants at their mothers' breasts, sat with me at the head of the table as we supped on boiled chicken and unlimited amounts of bread, cheese, and new ale. The talk was merry, and, truth be told, a lot of the men, including me, got more than a little tipsy. Anne was never mentioned.

Only one thing came up during our meal that raised my eyebrows—the Earl of Devon. The retired archer who spied for us whilst he poured bowls of ale in his Exeter alehouse had reported that the Earl had returned from exile in France four weeks ago. Unfortunately, he did not know why, only that a surprising number of mounted and seaborne couriers have been coming and going with messages ever since the earl returned.

Hmm. Something is up. On the other hand, Devon is almost certainly still on King John's list of enemies just as he is on ours. So maybe we can kill him now that he is back and take over Exeter Castle. Having it would help guard the approaches to Cornwall and push our frontier further out.

"Um, Thomas," I said as I leaned over the table and spoke quietly to my priestly brother, "is there any way you can find out how the king would react if we should happen to kill Devon and take Exeter Castle?"

"He might be pleased since Devon is one of his enemies," was Thomas's reply. "I will ask Albert if I can get a message to him." Albert, of course, being 'Father Alberto,' one of Thomas's students whom we had bribed into the household of the papal nuncio to be our spy at Windsor.

George was sitting next to Helen and overheard us. He leaned over and listened intently. So did Helen and Tori, even though, of course, I only talked to them in private about such matters.

Later Helen came to my bed in the corner of the sleeping room and washed me all over with a wet rag in the eastern way. She also trimmed my hair and beard with the two attached knives she brought back from Lisbon a couple of years ago, and brought me a new Egyptian tunic gown on to which she Tori had already sewed my stripes.

When she finished, she giggled and told me she had played "throw fingers" with her sister to see who would get to rub my back and wash me with wet rags on my first night home. That is something the women do for their men in the east where she and Tori had been birthed. So far, knock on wood, getting washed had not weakened me as I had been warned it might.

I got a playful smack on my ear and an "oh, you old devil" when I asked, "did you win or lose?"

She is alright, Helen is; she and Tori and their sister, Anne, were the best gifts I ever got from the Holy Land merchants who use our cogs and galleys. We three have been married up all right and proper ever since the children started coming.

Chapter Three

We get ready to fight.

The next morning there was a long line of men and women waiting to use the two piss pots in the castle's middle bailey. The line was so long and I was so desperate that I did not even try to climb the stone steps to use one of the shite holes at the top of the third curtain wall; I hurried out of the castle and peed against a tree growing just beyond the third moat.

I was not the only one who rushed out of the castle to pee. It was not surprising; my brother was very particular about where everyone dropped their piss and shite, and no one wanted to be on the receiving end of Thomas's fury. *He is very peculiar and hard to understand, my brother is; he claims the parchment books and scrolls he read in the monastery said Romans pissed and shite that way and they fielded armies and built roads and such for almost a thousand years.*

Afterwards, I felt much relieved and walked back to the middle bailey to get an onion and some bread, cheese, and a bowl of morning ale at the cookhouse. Peter was there and gave me a knowing and sympathetic smile when he saw me coming back over the second drawbridge. So did several of the sergeants standing in the line to get food and morning ale for themselves and their families.

There was no surprise in their smiles; they all knew Thomas's strange fixation about where everyone should piss and shite. They put it down to the fact that his mind was overfilled because he was both an archer lieutenant and a priest who could scribe and gobble church-talk.

I did not smile back; I would have done so, but I had not seen their smiles because I was so deep in thought about a decision I had finally made as I walked back to the cookhouse.

"Peter," I quietly announced as I walked up to him. "I am going to send to Okehampton for Raymond.

"The cat is out of the sack about the relics being in Cornwall. So it is time to send parchments out to the princes letting them know that we have the relics and telling them what they will have to do, and have to pay, in order to get them. Before I do though, I am going to call all the company's lieutenants and senior sergeants together to talk about what we should do to protect ourselves now that everyone knows we have the relics here at Restormel."

Peter nodded and started to respond, but then we got distracted when a hissing and snarling fight broke out between a couple of castle cats who had come to see if they could mooch a free breakfast instead of having to hunt for a mouse or a rat.

******

Three days later, late on a damp and misty afternoon, Raymond rode in from Okehampton with two of his men. My lieutenants and senior sergeants and I spent the entire next day considering the sale of the relics and how we should conduct it. We talked about everything from how and where to safely exchange them for the princes' coins, to who might attack us and how we would fight them.

My men were conflicted and so was I, and there was no doubt about it. Some of us thought that if there was an effort to take the relics by force, it would most likely to come from the sea; others that it would most likely come by land. We just did not know. All we knew was that a lot of powerful princes wanted the relics and we had in the room above the great hall.

We all agreed that the safest place for each relic's sale to take place would be from a heavily armed galley in the Fowey estuary with our other galleys standing nearby to defend it if necessary. The big question, however, was whether we should keep our men on the galleys at the mouth of the river to guard against a seaborne attacking force, or should they be formed up at Restormel or Launceston, or even across the border at Okehampton, so we would be ready to fight on land? Our men could not be everywhere at the same time. So where should we assemble them?

Raymond made a good point—whether by land or sea, we needed to get as much warning as possible before the enemy arrives so we can be ready to give them a warm welcome. That meant, he said, we should be sending some of his outriders from Okehampton further out along the roads in Devon and Somerset so that we would have at least a two or three day's warning if the king's army, or anyone else's, is coming to try to take them from us by force.

Thomas agreed with Raymond and similarly suggested that, because the European princes now know we have the relics the Pope wants, we also need advance warning if anyone brings an army by sea that might be used to take them.

"We can rely on the old archers spying for us in our Harfleur tavern to give us an early warning if the French once again begin assembling transports. But what if the Germans or Swedes bring an army when they come for the relics?

"It is a very real possibility, so we also need to station a couple of our fastest galleys to act as "outriders" at a port or ports where the northern princes would almost certainly stop for food and water on their way to Cornwall."

Worrying about someone sending an army to take the relics was obviously something Thomas had thought about before Raymond even brought it up, for he promptly unrolled a parchment map and tapped his finger on a village called Haarlem in the swampy lowlands of the Hollands.

"This is probably the best place to put them," he told us.

My brother was probably right because he had read so many books while he was in the monastery, more than ten to hear him tell it, but I was wishing Harold had been here to advise us instead of having gone out to our post on Cyprus; him being the lieutenant in charge of our cogs and galleys.

By the end of our day-long meeting, we had decided to send two galleys with extra rowers, but without archers, to wait and watch at Haarlem and also to immediately begin sending some of Raymond's outriders further out into Devon and Somerset to watch the roads. We also decided to send a fishing boat to Harfleur to alert the two archers we have stationed there. It would wait and carry back any warning messages.

Expanding the lands patrolled by Raymond's horse archers was an easy decision even though heretofore they would mostly been used to watch along the borders of Cornwall and our Okehampton Castle lands in Devon. We also talked about establishing some kind of caravan serais or alehouses along the road, nice ones that would attract the leaders of any forces coming towards Devon and Cornwall and let us weaken their tongues with drink the way we do in Exeter and Harfleur. *I had a few special thoughts about how they should look and be built, but I kept them to myself; we did not have time to build them.*

The next day, Raymond returned to Okehampton with his men. A few hours later four galleys fully crewed with sailors and rowed by some of our construction workers and villagers, but no archers, left with parchments asking the kings and princes to confirm that they were ready to buy the relics and telling them how we intended to proceed to sell them. One galley was sent to each of the four European princes who received parchments from the Pope. We would deal with the crusader lords later.

Raymond did not go home alone. He had surprised us by reporting that our herd of riding horses had grown such that he was once again short of archers who knew how to stay on a horse without falling off. Accordingly, George and one of Thomas's hurriedly ordained older students went with him to be Raymond's apprentice sergeant and scribe. So did thirty one-stripe and two-stripe archers who claimed to know how to ride a horse or, at least, were willing to be learnt.

Those of the men going with Raymond who did not yet have a horse to ride, and that was most of them, rode on top of the cargos in a long convoy of wains taking additional supplies of food and arrows to Okehampton. We were building up the castle's siege supplies so it would be ready in case there was fighting that resulted in a prolonged siege. They would probably get there about sundown on Friday if the weather held and Raymond pushed them.

I thought about what we had decided as I stood in our training camp next to the river and watched my son and the rest of Raymond's reinforcements leave for

Okehampton. One problem with no clear answer was that both of the German princes, Otto and Frederick, each wanted to buy the relics and donate them to the Church so the Pope would bless his claim to have been elected the Holy Roman Emperor.

At first, we were going to do what Cardinal Bertoli suggested and let the two Germans bid against each other so we would get the highest possible price for the relics. After we talked it over amongst ourselves, however, we had long ago decided to let them bid against each other so we would get the highest possible price—and then tell each of them that he had won the bidding, collect his coins, and give him some of the relics. That way we would get all the coins each of them was willing to pay to become the Emperor, and they would each have some relics to donate to the Church.

Thomas had suggested the idea of letting them both win the bidding. He thought the Pope would like it. Indeed, he said he was so sure Cardinal Bertoli and the Pope would like it, because they would get more coins for themselves, that he assured us we could safely proceed as if we had already received their approval.

"I mean, really, so what if a few more princes are allowed to escape purgatory if it benefits the Church?" said Thomas.

Not everyone understood.

"But there is only one emperor for the Holy Roman Empire. The Pope cannot give his blessing to both of them, can he?" asked Peter with a hint of disbelief in his voice.

"Do not worry about it," was my priestly brother's reply as he took a big bite of chicken and gave a little belch.

"The Pope is a smart man and he needs the money. He will surely come up with something to keep them both happy."

****** *George*

We saw Okehampton Castle in the distance as we came through the woods on the muddy and rutted cart path that runs up to the castle from the old Roman road running between London and Exeter. It is a lovely place and very defensible. The men were very excited to see it, as well they should be. It will be their home for some years if they did not get cut down or die of some pox.

I knew Okehampton because I had been here several times before—the first time as a young boy when my father and the archers killed the Courtney lord and took it for Cornwall. It had all been very exciting. I had stood behind our men with four other of the older boys from Uncle Thomas's school, and even loosed three arrows from my small bow over the heads of our men when the lord of the castle and his men charged them. Courtney had done so thinking my father and his men were a bunch of defenceless travellers who could not fight back because they were not wearing armour.

The second time I saw it was a couple of years ago when I was a young apprentice sergeant. I was in a battle on this very road when Sir William Brereton and his men tried to take the relief wains bringing corn and dried fish to Okehampton during the great famine. It was the first time I actually commanded men in battle—twenty-two newly trained archers who had been pressed into service as wain drivers to help get the famine food distributed.

It had been a hard fight, and we would have lost if Lieutenant Raymond and some of his horse archers had not arrived in time to stand with us. Together we killed almost all of Brereton's men and set the rest to helping row one of our galleys to the Holy Land. I have been partial to the horse archers ever since.

"Does it bring back memories, George?" asked Lieutenant Raymond as he pulled his horse to a walk next to mine.

"Aye Uncle Raymond, that it does." *All the company's original archers are my uncles even though my only real uncle is Uncle Thomas who learnt me to do my sums and read and jabber in Latin. It has been that way ever since I was a young boy and they helped my father carry me over the wall and away from Lord Edmund's castle when the Saracens overran it.*

"Well lad, you have the four stripes of a company sergeant now and rightly so, and you are damn lucky to be alive if half of what I heard about the battle with the French is true."

"I was too busy swimming clear of the wreckage to be scared, Uncle Raymond, as God is my witness. Afterwards, when I got to thinking about it, I shook like a wet dog."

"Well, you are not to take such chances out here. You will be sergeanting the outriders I will be sending out into Devon and Somerset on the London road. A couple of my best three-stripe file sergeants and their chosen men will be going with you, so you should be alright.

"Just be sure to listen to your sergeants, and remember your job is only to do whatever damage you can safely do and send couriers back to warn us that danger is coming; it is not for you to stand and fight like a hero and get yourself killed or captured for ransom."

******

Okehampton Castle was quite impressive with its two great curtain walls and battlements standing out against the sky. I pulled up my horse at the village at the foot of the castle's hill and drank it all in—and wondered how long it would be my home. At least until the relics are sold, I would imagine. I should have asked my father if I could bring Beth or Becky with me.

We received a fine welcome as we clattered over the second drawbridge and rode into the inner bailey. The people in the castle had seen us coming up the path and rushed out to greet us. Servants and archers immediately came into the bailey to hold our horses and present us with the traditional bowls of arrival ale.

I had seen Lady Isabel several times previously and immediately recognized her when she came into the bailey. From listening to my father and uncle I knew a secret that most people did not know and never would—with Uncle Thomas's help as the Bishop of Cornwall, she had somehow married Lord Courtney and we had bought Okehampton off him *after* he died.

She must have asked someone who I was because she smiled and walked over to me.

"Hoy and God's blessings on you, sergeant—why you are George are you not you, William's son? And now you are all grown up and a company sergeant with four stripes; my goodness, how time flies!" She said it with both pleasure and sadness in her voice.

"Hoy and God's blessings on you, Lady Isabel. Yes, it is me, George. My father said that I was to give you his warmest regards."

"Oh thank you for telling me. And this is my son, his name is William too."

Chapter Four

The gathering storm

Okehampton was as a nice a place for an archer to live as one could hope to find. It was all highly organized and very modern. Lady Isabel and her son and servant lived in one of the two rooms above the castle's great hall with its big fireplace and long wooden table; Raymond lived in the other with Wanda, his wife with the strange eyes from the land on the other side of the Saracens' great desert.

The horse archers themselves, and the women they had attracted, lived with their horses in the outer bailey in hovels built all along outer curtain wall. They spent from dawn to dusk every day gathering food for their horses and being learnt and re-learnt to push out their arrows and to ride and fight in various ways. In return, they got their hovels to live in, their weapons and horses, and two big meals each day for themselves and their families, all in addition to their annual pay and any prize monies they might earn.

Raymond's senior sergeant, his two four-stripe company sergeants, and his eleven or twelve three-stripe file sergeants, patrol sergeants as Raymond called them, lived in the turrets along the wall in the inner bailey. That was where I as a new four-stripe sergeant expected to live. It was not to be.

"You can sleep in the hall tonight, George. But you are not to make yourself at home. Tomorrow I want you to take a couple of files of our outriders down the London road to watch for signs of trouble. Go down the road a good four days march on foot from Okehampton and camp well off the road where you cannot be seen. Do you understand?"

"Aye, Uncle, I understand. A good four days walk and camp off the road."

"Good. I will be sending out a similar force under Michael the mason to watch the Exeter road." *We have so many Michaels who have made their marks on the company roll that we have to scribe something special about them so we can tell them apart. Michael Mason was probably a mason's apprentice before he went for an archer.*

"I will expect both of you to send a rider to me every day with a report of what you have seen even if you have seen nothing. Do you understand?"

"Aye, Uncle, I understand. I will send a report to you every day."

"Good. Now we must go to supper. Lady Isabel asked that you join us."

******

The next morning was all hustle and bustle.

"Stand ready," a company sergeant cried as Uncle Raymond and I walked up to the men who would be going with me on the London road. The men were already standing one behind the other in two seven-man fighting files as was the custom for inspections. They stiffened even more at the sergeant's order.

Our horses were off to the side being held by some of the stable boys. With each of them was something that the outriders did not usually take with them when they went out on a patrol and might need to ride fast—a sturdy supply horse for each file. It would be led by one of the outriders and carry a leather tent, a cooking pot, a knight's breastplate that had been hammered flat so it could be laid on a campfire to cook flat bread, and various food supplies and additional arrows.

The additional equipment, supplies, and arrows were significant; it meant we would be away for an extended period of time. Our long, hooded rain skins, as always, were rolled up and tied behind our saddles.

Uncle Raymond introduced me to my two file sergeants and their chosen men, one of whom I immediately recognized because he had been with me as a one-stripe archer when we freed the slaves at the tin mine during the great famine. *And once again the dear man did it in a very supportive way to give me credibility and instant acceptance.*

"This here is Sergeant George. Him and me go back a long ways—we went o'er the wall together when the God-cursed Saracens overran Edmund's castle long before any of you lot even knew our company existed. I am telling you this because some of you are going to be daft and think you can play tricks on him when you find out he is also a priest because he was learnt in Bishop Thomas's school to scribe and gobble in church-talk.

"I would leave you to try your tricks so he and I could get a good laugh, but we have no time for that because we need to get an early warning if any enemies come up the London Road to try to take our relics. It could be dangerous because you will be going out beyond our own lands.

"So try to keep this behind your eyes in your empty heads—Sergeant George here has stood firm and fought in more battles than any of you lot, and probably killed more of our enemies than all of you put together. So do what he tells you and you will be alright."

Then he gave me a big smile, clapped me on the shoulder most manly-like, and walked away. I knuckled my head with a respectful salute as he did. *Time to start.*

"Alright lads, get ready to show me your weapons and bowstrings."

* * * * * *

Before I started the inspection, I told the men how pleased I was to have a chance to serve with them because I knew they were all outriders, the men who went out in pairs to scout in front of our forces and watch our borders, the best of the best. Then I had one of the two lines of men take two paces to the side so I could walk between them and inspect their weapons.

I shook the hand of each man as I came to him and had him tell me his name as he showed me his longbow, quivers and arrows, knife, and bowstrings including the spare we all carried under our knitted cap to keep it dry. I started with a man I recognized.

"Alfred, it is you, by God; and a chosen man with two stripes. It is good to see you, it certainly is. I am pleased we will be together. I remember how you put an arrow damn near all the way through that big slave driver who tried to attack us at the tin mine, I surely do. It was a damn fine shot, it surely was."

"Hoy, George, and it is good to see you too," Alfred said with a shy smile as he wiped his hand on his tunic and shook mine. He was more than a little pleased to be recognized in front of his mates.

Acknowledging that they were all outriders, the best of the best, and my recognizing of Alfred seemed to greatly please the men. I could tell as I briefly stopped to talk to each man and check his weapons. I did not quite understand their pleasure, but I had seen it before and felt it myself; elite fighting men like to be recognized and appreciated by their sergeants, and rightly so.

In any event, my inspection went quickly and well. Everyone was ready except for one poor sod who got shouted at and cuffed on his ear by his file sergeant for not having an extra bowstring under his cap. Within minutes we were saddling our horses and getting ready to ride. Mine was a big black ambler with his bollocks chopped off.

I could sense that the men were excited about going off to do something new and unknown that might have a whiff of danger to it; so was I. I really like being a sergeant.

Raymond and a number of the castle's women came out to see us off and were standing in the outer bailey as we rode out of the castle. They raised their hands in friendly salutes as we clattered out over the outer drawbridge with our longbows in one hand and our reins in the other. I lifted my bow in acknowledgement and so did some of the men.

If no one tried to stop us, and we rode steadily down the old Roman road towards London, we should be able to get a good two days walk from Okehampton by sundown even if we do not push our horses, which we would not do in order to keep them fresh in case we come across some trouble. Our plan was to continue riding on towards London the next morning until we had travelled the distance it would take a man two days to walk, and then try to find a safe place to camp. It looked like it was going to rain again.

******

We began meeting roadside pedlars and a constant stream of travellers going in both directions as soon as we reached the end of the cart path running up to the castle and moved on to the old Roman road that runs between London and Exeter. The only traveller who raised any questions in my mind was a fast-moving galloper we met after we had been on the road for a while. He ignored my friendly hail and rode past us without even slowing down or saying a word.

The people we met were travelling normally, though some got a bit fearful when they saw our large group of armed men riding together. The same with the roadside pedlars; sometimes they gathered up their apples and turnips and such and hurried away as we approached.

A couple of hours after we reached the London road, a group of pilgrims, probably walking to a shrine somewhere, panicked at seeing a large group of armed men coming towards them and ran off the road to escape from us.

Enough. We were scaring people and calling too much attention to ourselves. From that point on I began spacing my men out along the road and rode ahead and alone so I could talk to the people I met or overtook. I would have cut across the fields to save time, but the road was so straight that I thought there was nothing to be gained by leaving it. Staying on the road turned out to be a huge mistake, and so was spreading my men out and riding out front all alone. It happened late the next morning after we had crossed into Somerset.

******

The previous night my men and I moved a ways off the road and camped near a little stream as the sun began to go down. We did not bother to set up our two tents because the rain did not last long and it did not look like more was in the offing. It was the end of a warm and uneventful day. I used my knife to scrape a hole in the ground for my hip, wrapped myself in my hooded, leather rain skin, and instantly fell asleep.

We broke camp the next morning as soon as the sun came up and resumed our march to get farther down the road towards London. I once again took the lead with my men strung out behind me every three or four hundred paces. I somehow had a thought behind my eyes that I should chat up everyone coming towards us to ask what they had seen along the way.

It was a somewhat cloudy day and all went well until we had been on the road for about three hours. An overloaded hay wain pulled by a pair of oxen was coming towards me on the road when all of sudden the ragged villager driving it stood up and pointed towards me with a look of alarm on his face. *At me? No.* I looked over my shoulder and saw commotion and disorder on the road behind me—my men, those that I could see, were galloping up the road towards me and moving fast.

I could not see behind them to understand why they were all coming at a hard gallop, but it could not be good. I immediately strung my longbow by leaning to the side of my horse and pressing one end of my bow on the ground to bend it while I slipped the bowstring on the other end. Then I nocked an arrow and waited. My horse had caught my excitement and pranced a bit as I moved off the road and stood in my stirrups in an effort to see what I might see.

* * * * * *

One after another, my outriders reached me and wheeled around to form a rough line off to my right as I motioned with my arm for them to do. Those who had not already done so, strung their bows. Behind them, in pursuit, came a dozen or so riders on bigger and slower horses, knights and their mounted squires and sergeants for sure. And behind them, in the distance, I could see a mob of running men on foot trying to catch up with the riders. A typical knight and his retainers.

"They got Charlie and our supply horse," one of the last of my men to arrive shouted excitedly as he wheeled his horse around and hurriedly strung his longbow.

"Ready your heavies, lads," I shouted as the on-coming horsemen approached. "Ready your heavies and pick your man. But do not push an arrow at them until I give the order, not a one." *Maybe I can avoid a fight was the thought in my mind.*

My sergeants and chosen men promptly and properly repeated my orders at the top of their voices as is the custom. Three or four of the men immediately returned their nocked arrows to one of the three quivers each outrider had slung over his shoulder and selected another.

I motioned with my hand for the men to stay in their rough line as I moved forward a few horse lengths to get in front of them to meet the oncoming riders. I kept my arrow nocked with one hand as I raised the other towards the oncoming horsemen with my palm open in the age-old signal to stop.

There was the briefest moment when I thought they would just keep coming and we would have to push our arrows at them without even knowing why we were fighting. But they slowed and brought their horses to a halt. There were almost as many of them as there were of us. About half of them appeared to be knights. Every man had either a drawn sword in his hand or was carrying a lance, and most of them looked like they might know how to use them.

A knight with a coat of arms of three bears on his shield walked his horse forward towards me and arrogantly named himself as Sir Joseph Temple of Dunster Castle—and demanded to know "who are you men and why are you carrying weapons in Somerset." He was an older man with flecks of grey in his beard. His sword was drawn.

"I am George, an archer from Cornwall," I said. "We are on our way to London to buy horses," I told my lie loudly so my men could hear me.

"And you? Why are you and your men attacking peaceful travellers on the king's road? One of my men is missing and so are two of my horses. I want them returned immediately."

"Do not make demands on your betters; you would not if you know what is good for you," was the knight's response with a threatening and arrogant tone in his voice and a wave of the sword he was holding. *He seemed to enjoy displaying his power to impress his men.*

While Sir Joseph was posturing, the first of his thirty or so puffing and gasping foot soldiers began to arrive and form themselves into a disorganized mob behind his dozen or so mounted men. Some of them were carrying swords and shields but others had only wooden spears. It was the typical village levy that a minor baron could put into the field; three or four poorly armed serfs or free men on foot for every rider.

The arrival of the knight's foot was something I appreciated though I doubt neither they nor Sir Joseph knew it or would understand why; I wanted them to arrive and join the mounted men in front of us so they would not be able to get away into the nearby woods if it came to a fight and we wanted to kill them all.

Sir Joseph's men listened to his arrogant words and seemed to enjoy them. They were smirking at the misfortune they thought had befallen us. So was Sir Joseph as the last of his men on foot reached us. They were all puffing and winded from their exertions.

Sir Joseph pulled his horse around in a tight circle so he could check on his arriving foot and then turned back to me with a satisfied look on his face. I could see that he and some of the other riders with him were wearing shirts of chain.

"He is dead, your man is, just as you will soon be if you do not surrender. We will settle for your horses and weapons and you can be on your way."

"You killed him? You are sure he is dead?" I asked incredulously. I was truly surprised.

"Of course, I am sure. Now get down from those horses and run off before I change my mind about letting you go."

I did not hesitate and I certainly did not respond as he expected. Sir Joseph and his men were still smirking as my bow came up and I pushed one of my armour-piercing heavies straight into the chain shirt covering his chest. As I did, I shouted "Push on them lads; shoot them down."

Sir Joseph was so close that I could not possibly miss, and I did not. The iron tip of my armour-piercing heavy caught him squarely in the chest and went in half way to its fletching despite the chain mail shirt he was wearing.

It was as if everything was happening very slowly. An instant later he was looking down at the goose feathers at the end of the shaft in stunned disbelief. That was when a second heavy from one of my men slammed into him and his horse bolted into mine. It almost knocked my horse down and me out of my saddle. My horse stumbled to the side and almost went down; I was lucky to recover without being dumped on to the ground.

My instant killing of Sir Joseph had caught the Dunster men totally by surprise. Even more importantly, my men had been ready to push out their arrows and had acted faster to get into the fight than the Dunster men, much faster.

There was little wonder in my men's fast and continuous response; it was something they had practised many times previously. My men began pouring their armour piercing heavies into the Dunster riders and their horses before the riders even had time to raise their shields. Many of them fell before they had a chance to kick their horses in the ribs to close with us and bring their swords and lances into the fight.

It was all over almost before it began. Most of the Dunster horsemen did not even have time to get to us with their swords and lances before they were hit or their grievously wounded horses went down or bolted. In the end, only one of the Dunster knights was able to cover the few feet separating us and reach our rough line of horsemen. He drove his lance deep into an archer's screaming horse and knocked it and its rider to the ground.

The knight either let loose of his lance as he went on past or it was pulled out of his hands by being stuck in the horse. It did not matter, he had just started to draw his sword and turn his horse to come back and join the melee when he was hit in the back and side by multiple arrows that knocked him all the way out of his saddle.

Some of the Dunster riders had kicked their horses in the ribs and started forward when they realized the fighting had started. But they were close and my outriders were fully ready with their arrows nocked and had already picked their man.

Most of the riders were hit immediately. A few recognized what was happening and instinctively began hauling hard on their horses' reins to turn them away in an effort to escape. It did not work for them. My outriders poured arrows into their unprotected backs and horses. Only one of the horsemen was able to successfully turn back to escape, and he knocked down some of the Dunster foot as he did.

"Get him," I shouted as my horse and I regained our balance and I pushed an arrow at the fleeing rider. He hunched down in his saddle and leaned to the left just as I pushed it at him, and I missed. But one or more of the three outriders who had begun galloping after him did not miss. The knight rode on for at least a hundred paces before he slowly slid off his saddle with his foot caught in the stirrup and his panic-stricken horse began dragging him in a big circle.

There were screaming and shouting men, bolting horses, and men on the ground everywhere in the open field next to the London road. My line of horse archers had been scattered and pushed every which way as the

Dunster horses with empty saddles and wounded riders bolted forward and crashed into them. Within a few brief seconds the Dunster horsemen had been destroyed almost to a man, and the Dunster foot were throwing down their weapons and running in every direction with the horse archers in hot pursuit and riding them down.

We needed prisoners to question, so I began shouting orders to stop the slaughter.

Chapter Five

We learn something surprising.

Many of the Dunster men we took as prisoners were wounded by the time I was able to stop the killing. Sir Joseph was dead and so were three or four of his riders. All the rest of the riders were wounded except two who were thrown off their wounded horses, several so severely that they would almost certainly need a mercy.

Few, if any, of the Dunster foot escaped into the nearby trees, and those we caught were mostly serfs who did not know anything except that their lord had ordered them to follow Sir Joseph.

The best that could be said of the Dunster men was that they were loyal to their lord even though they were poorly trained and equipped. After we stripped them of their weapons, and the helmets the riders and a couple of the Dunster foot were wearing, I told the Dunster foot to look after each other and their wounded and go home. I also invited them to walk to Cornwall with their families and become apprentice archers if they wanted to be free men and coin-earning soldiers.

I kept the riders.

Two of the riders we took prisoner were knights whose horses went down. Of the others, one was Sir Joseph's young squire, a boy much too young to be taken into a battle, and three were sergeants, one of whom looked to be an experienced veteran. The two knights could not understand what had happened. We were, after all, just commoners and did not even wear armour.

One of the unwounded knights, the young one, was immediately so arrogant and disrespectful that I seriously considered letting the archers use him for target practice. They were all soon willing to tell us whatever we wanted to know. They started when the young one initially refused to talk to me and I ordered one of my sergeants to begin cutting off his fingers one joint at a time as the Saracens do when they want their questions answered. It only took the loss of one joint to start him babbling.

The squire turned out to be the most helpful of all. He was a young lad and became absolutely terrified as he watched James cut off part of the young knight's finger and the knight began screaming and sobbing and telling us all he knew. The young squire was particularly helpful because he would have been present when Sir Joseph had been given his orders by the Dunster baron.

I listened intently as the terrified boy told me what he would have heard when Sir Joseph got his orders. After I had asked him a good many questions because what he told me was so alarming, I ordered two of the archers to get ready to ride hard to Okehampton with an urgent message and to take the young squire with them so he could be additionally questioned—"and bring back a couple of cheeses and a stringer of chickens or geese if you can get them."

While I was listening to the young squire and trying to confirm what he would told me with the other Dunster riders, the archers had been busy stripping the dead men and our prisoners of their clothes and weapons and going up the road to look for Charlie and the supply horse he had been leading.

We found Charlie's body with our missing supply horse grazing nearby. His riding horse was gone. We never did find it and Charlie was our only death. All we knew was that he would have been leading his file's supply horse and bringing up the rear when the Dunster men came up the road behind us.

Charlie had apparently tried to escape when he finally realized their murderous intent but could not get the supply horse to run fast enough. He should have dropped its reins and fled, but he did not. It was Charlie's shouts and effort to flee that had alerted the others and sent them galloping down the road to join me.

My two messengers hurriedly left, leading a horse with the young squire tied to its saddle. Each was riding one of the newly captured Dunster horses and leading his own to keep it fresh in case he ran into more trouble and had to run for it. After they left, we had the prisoners dig a grave and buried poor Charlie where he fell. The men took off their caps and were somber, but seemed quite pleased when I gobbled a few prayers in Latin to help send poor Charlie on his way.

There remained only the five captured riders to deal with. We had kept them separate from the others and had not freed them when we sent the Dunster foot home carrying their wounded. Now I had to decide what to do with them. Killing the prisoners was not an option even though Charlie's sergeant suggested we should and offered to do it. Not a chance, I told him rather huffily; we do not want to ever get a reputation of killing prisoners because it would discourage surrenders.

Besides, I had never hear the end of it from Uncle Thomas.

****

All of the travellers and pedlars on the road had either hurried away or disappeared into the nearby woods as soon as the fighting started. There was no trace of them except for a wain with two oxen in its traces that had been abandoned on the road with a great load of hay.

One of the archers used his knife to cut strips of linen from the tunic of one of the dead knights. We used them to tie the arms of four of our remaining prisoners behind their backs. The fifth was not tied. It was not necessary. He had two arrows in him and was in such agony that I considered letting one of his friends kill him as an act of mercy; he would not be a threat.

While the prisoners were being examined and tied, I had some of my men unload the hay and throw the prisoners and captured arms and saddles into the wain while others of them removed the oxen pulling it and replaced them with two of the captured horses. We took the rest of the captured horses with us for use as remounts. One of the archers picked up an apple left behind by a fleeing roadside pedlar and began eating it.

He offered to cut a piece for me but I was too busy and too excited to be hungry.

Two very frightened and ragged serfs came out of the woods while we were loading the prisoners into the wain. They hesitantly approached us, and got down on their knees in front of me and began gobbling a local dialect I could hardly understand. They were obviously a father and son.

It was obviously their master's wain and the father was terribly afraid of what would happen to him and his son "who is much too small to be whipped and beaten and might be sold" if they lost the wain and the oxen.

"Well, we cannot have that, can we?" I said once I understood.

"Alright then; you can drive the wain with the prisoners to Okehampton and bring it back to your master when we are finished with it."

The man seemed relieved to the point of tears when he understood my words; he tried to kiss my hands and put my foot on his head. They must have a terrible master. It moved some of my men as well. Immediately afterwards, I noticed two of them talking intensely to the father and pointing in the direction of Cornwall.

A few minutes later the wain started its long trip to Okehampton with three outriders riding along side of the wain as its guards. The prisoners and the serf driving the wain did not know it, of course, but I had told the chosen man in charge of the patrol to immediately abandon the wain and its cargo if they run into trouble. If they do, they are either to ride back here or for Okehampton, whichever they think they would most likely reach safely.

I was deep in thought as my eight remaining men and I mounted our horses and once again began to move down the road towards where I had been told to establish a watching camp. We left as soon as the wain and its dispirited cargo of prisoners headed off in the other direction towards Okehampton and their uncertain future.

We left the dead Dunster men and their knight for the crows.

****** *Lieutenant Raymond at Okehampton*

George's latest message was a great surprise and quite shocking; and, after a few words with the outriders who brought it to me and the captured squire from Dunster, I was sure it was true. The Earl of Devon was gathering some the dissident barons together to march against Cornwall. The young squire he would captured did not know why or how many. I was fairly sure I knew why; it was almost certainly an effort to seize the relics before we had a chance to sell them.

I talked things over with my wife, Wanda, as I always tried to do before I make a decision or send a message. *She is from beyond the great desert and very good at thinking in her head.*

Wanda pointed out that I could not be sure of anything. All I knew for sure was that at least one of the dissident barons was on his way to join up with the Earl of Devon and that a party of men led by one of the baron's knights attacked George and his men.

If the squire was telling the truth, and I was rather sure that he was, it had been a king's messenger on his way from London to Devon who had reported the presence of George and his men heading eastbound on the London road. Sir Joseph and his men had been sent to see who they were and what they were doing. But why had Sir Joseph and his men attacked George and his outriders? It was all very confusing.

In any event, my wife and I agreed that Captain William needed to know all this as soon as possible. I immediately had my new apprentice sergeant scribe a parchment reporting what had happened and sent two gallopers to deliver it to William at Restormel.

I asked Wanda what she thought William would make of my report and what he would do when he read it? She did not know.

Chapter Six

Who is coming for the relics?

Raymond did exactly the right thing when George sent in his message reporting his battle with the Dunster men, and what he would learnt from the men he captured—he sent a pair of gallopers straight to me to tell me all about it. I immediately summoned my available lieutenants, Thomas, Peter and Henry, and read them the message.

We could not be certain what it was all about. That was what my lieutenants and I decided after we talked it over. But it would appear that King John may have made peace with Devon and the barons, and agreed to grant them some of the things they wanted if they would get the relics so he could send them to the Pope. It was the only possible explanation—unless the barons were acting on behalf of Phillip of France or someone we did not know about. Why else would the barons and their men be gathering to attack us?

****** *George*

My greatly reduced force of outriders, eight men plus myself, continued on down the road after our fight with the Dunster knight and his men. We had lost almost an entire day, but our basic assignment, to watch the road for armies moving towards Cornwall, was not changed by our fight with the Dunster men or the information we had tortured out of our prisoners.

If anything, or so it seemed to me, watching the road and reporting on its travellers became even more important. In any event, my men were quite chuffed by our victory and began loudly telling each other all about it and what they had seen and done. Truth be told, I was fairly chuffed myself.

My men and I camped well off the London road on the night of the battle with the Dunster men and continued moving eastward at sunup the next morning. Everything was normal along the road the next day, except that everyone we met already knew about the fighting and asked us about it.

Travellers fleeing the scene, it seems, had spread the word about the battle. It grew in size as we moved further and further away from the battle site until the breathless accounts from the travellers we met, to say nothing of the drinkers in the alehouses and the roadside pedlars along the way, had many armies involved and foretold the end of days.

The people we met seemed quite taken aback, even disappointed, when they heard our version of the story—that there had been an incident on the road with some robbers and they had been quickly put down even though, quite sadly, we had lost a man in the process. We were, we assured everyone who inquired, continuing on our way to Hathersage and London on our annual trip to get horses for our riders and increase our herd of brood mares.

******

Two exhausted gallopers bringing messages and supplies from Okehampton caught up with us on the second day after the battle. The gallopers came in on lathered horses with a staggering supply horse loaded with the cheeses and two flapping and squawking strings of the chickens I had requested. They reached us just as we were turning off the London road to set up a permanent camp on a hillside overlooking it.

It is a good thing the gallopers found us when they did; they would have missed us and continued on down the road if they had arrived ten minutes later. Their arrival increased my force to a total of eleven horse archers including me.

I did not lead my men and the two gallopers straight to the area I had selected for a campsite when we turned off the road. To the contrary, because there were a number of travellers and pedlars on the road watching, I led my little band up a little valley on the south side of the road—and then, much later, by the light of the almost full moon, we circled all the way around in the dark and re-crossed the road to reach the distant hillside site I had chosen north of the road. We had watch the road from here.

And we had watch from the other side of the road as well. I left two of the outriders and their horses on a hill on the south side of the road. They were to stay there out of sight, and ride for Okehampton to report if we were attacked and driven out of our main camp.

******

The messages the two gallopers brought in from Okehampton merely repeated what I had already been ordered to do by Uncle Raymond—continue to watch the road and every day send a courier in with a report as to what we have seen and heard. So that was what we did. Early the next day, before the sun came up, I sent a single rider to Okehampton with a report. I had him awake and on the road before daylight so no one would be able to know from whence he would come.

My courier always rode one saddled horse and led another; and he rode light carrying only one quiver of arrows, a water skin, his longbow, and a small sack of oats for his horses. If he rode hard, and was not delayed or intercepted, he should be able to make it to Okehampton by late that night or early the next morning.

******

Each day for the next three days, two gallopers arrived and I sent one of my men back with a "nothing important to report" message. The only significant message I received was a parchment order from my father on the second day—if we come across another armed party, and we are certain it is heading for Cornwall, my men and I are to immediately send a warning message and commence picking off the enemy couriers and foragers whenever we can safely take them.

We were, in other words, to begin doing as much damage to the enemy as possible, and keep it up for as long as possible. In the meantime, a messenger was to continue to be sent to Okehampton each day even if there was nothing of importance to report.

I immediately assembled my men and read the order to them—and promptly began worrying about the two archers on the big hill across from us who would not know what to do.

The next two days were idyllic and boring. We sat in the shade and watched the road, picked our teeth with blades of grass, and looked after our horses and our clothes and weapons. We also made some ancient weapons—sharpened wooden spears and a couple of old fashioned battle hammers with a large stone attached to the end of a cleft stick using strips of leather.

Each day two messengers arrived and each day I sent one messenger back to Okehampton with a "nothing special to report" report. I made no effort to contact the men on the hill on the other side of the road. I did not want to alert the pedlars and travellers on the road that we had two posts watching it.

I could have sent out two messengers each morning, of course, but I decided one man leading a spare horse had a better chance of getting through. Besides, it let me build up the number of men under my command to ten plus the two men on the hill on the other side of the road.

******

Everything changed on the fourth day after our battle with the Dunster men. It occurred four or five hours after I had sent off the day's messenger in the early morning hours to once again report that everything was quiet.

It was late in the morning and I was leaning back against a tree and snoozing when I first heard our lookout's excited call from down at the edge of the woods.

"Hoy, Sergeant. Riders on the road to the east. Looks like a lot of them and they are coming this way. Maybe soldiers on foot as well, but I am not sure yet. Please come quick."

I started down the tree-covered hill towards the lookouts and so, quite dangerously, did all the rest of my men.

"Everyone stay where you are. Sergeants and chosen men, see to it." I shouted. Then I added a bit of explanation. "We do not want them to see everyone moving about and know we are up here."

Then I pointed at Samuel, one of my two file sergeants, and motioned with a "come on" motion of my hand for him to follow me. We hurried through the trees on the hill to the tree line and crept in next to our lookouts who were crouched down behind a fallen tree at the edge of the woods.

Once we were in place, Samuel and I carefully and slowly raised our heads to look at the road running through the valley below us. *Of course, we raised them slowly; every experienced soldier knows it is movement that attracts the eye. Uncle Thomas made much of it when he was putting the learning on us in his school.*

What I saw coming down the road towards us from the east was instantly recognizable for what it was—an army on the move towards Devon and Cornwall. There were hundreds of them, thousands more likely. The column soon stretched out along the road for as far as I could see. Travellers on the road below us were hurrying into the fields and forests on either side of the road to get out of its way.

What I did not see were any outriders scouting for enemies out in front of the column or off to its side. Whoever it was, they thought they had nothing to fear.

"Have you seen any outriders come past?" I inquired of the two lookouts as I settled in next to them. I looked at them keenly as I asked. It was an important question.

"No sergeant," said the lookout closest to me, a chosen man with two stripes on his tunic gown. It was Alfred who had fought by my side at the tin mine. I smiled at him and gave him a nod of recognition.

"The damn fools. Well, they will pay for that mistake." *I said it loudly so all three of the men, not just Alfred, could hear; I wanted it to get back to the rest of my men so they had know we had be fighting an incompetently led army and their spirits would rise.*

As the riders at the head of the column came closer and closer I could see that the army, for that was certainly what it was, was quite large, moving slowly, and very disorganized. In many ways, it was as if it was a long column of many different small armies instead of one large one.

I finally realized as the slow-moving army got closer and closer, that there were separate mini-armies of various sizes being led by lords and knights on horseback. Each lord was independently leading his own force of knights and retainers behind his own banner.

What I had not yet seen, at least not so far, was a great gathering of mounted men with banners or a huge retinue of toadies and guards such as I would expect to see if King John or the leader of his army, William

Marshall, were present. Maybe they are in the back of the column or will come later.

I had seen enough, however, and I wanted my messengers to get on the road safely ahead of the men in the slowly moving column. I motioned for Samuel to follow me as I slid backwards for a few feet and then turned around and ran through the trees until I reached the rest of my men. Before I did, however, I told Alfred and the other lookouts to start counting the mounted men and to put one stone in a pile for every ten knights and armed horsemen who rode or led a horse past us.

"And do not forget to include those who are walking and leading their horses or having a servant do it."

* * * * * *

"Fred, Guy." I shouted as I ran up to my anxiously waiting men, all of whom were seeing to their horses and preparing for a rapid departure. "Each of you two take a spare horse as a remount and ride for Okehampton as fast as possible. Split up and travel on alone if you run into trouble. Do not stop until you reach the castle.

"Tell the Lieutenant that there is a large army, thousands of men and horses, on the road and moving slowly, very slowly, towards Devon and Cornwall. Tell him I said they are not likely to reach the turnoff to Okehampton for five or six days unless they speed up.

"Also tell him they appear to be very disorganized with each baron leading his own men and that they do not have outriders out to warn against attacks, although that may change once we start picking off their foragers and stragglers. Also, and this is important, tell him that, at least so far, there is no sign of the king or any of the king's men."

"Good man, Fred." I said as he leaned down from his saddle to string his bow and then grabbed the reins of his remount. "Be careful and go with God. You too, Guy."

I held up the little wooden cross I wear on a string around my neck, mumbled a few words of Latin, and made the sign of the cross to bless them as Guy finished tightening his remount's saddle and swung himself up on to his riding horse in one smooth motion. The rest of the men were very excited and looked at me expectantly.

"The rest of you stay here and get your horses saddled and ready to leave on a moment's notice. And get our lookouts' horses ready for them, and the supply horses as well."

Those were the orders I gave as I watched Fred and Guy ride out of our camp leading their remounts and begin moving as fast as they could through the densely packed trees. They moving through the trees as fast as possible, and rightly so, because they understand that they need to get ahead of the army below us so they can ride on the road.

Then I hurried down through the forest to re-join our lookouts and once again watch the army passing below us.

When I got back to our lookouts, I could see the column more closely as it began to pass directly in front of me. There was a clear pattern—each of the barons was leading his own little army of knights and mounted men with his poorly armed servants and serfs walking behind them.

The pile of stones in front of our lookouts was already large and it was rapidly growing.

******

We watched for hours as the barons and their men slowly passed on the road below us. As would be expected, there were four or five men on foot for every mounted man. They looked to be mostly the poorly armed men of village levies. Following along behind them was a long baggage train of wains and a large number of camp followers, both riding and walking, but mostly walking.

The baggage train stretched out behind the fighting men for as far as I could see. It was an army on the move for sure—and it did not at all look as if it was prepared to fight off an attack. If I had had a larger force of archers, I could have burst out of the trees and destroyed them all as I had watched my father do years ago from the Trematon Castle keep when it was attacked. *But I do not have such a force; so my men and I will have to settle for doing what we can do.*

There was still no sign of the king or any of his men.

Chapter Seven

My fears are confirmed.

Our horses were saddled and ready as the sun began coming up and my men gathered around me to get their orders. There were eight men listening as I told them what we had be doing and what I expected of them. We had already eaten a big breakfast of flatbread, cheese, and burnt chicken strips, and scattered the ashes of the cooking fire we had use to bake the bread. In addition to our longbows and quivers, each of us was carrying his newly made wooden spear and stone battle hammer, and had one or more extra bales of arrows lashed on behind his saddle.

"Listen up lads. It is almost certain where that lot down on the road is heading—to lay siege to Okehampton Castle and then continue on to attack Cornwall and seize the relics before they can be sold. If that happens, none of will get our prize money. So it is our job to slow them down and weaken them by attacking their baggage train, and then begin picking off their stragglers and preventing them from foraging or receiving supplies.

"To start with, now that their main force has passed, we are going to fall in with the baggage train on the road and act as if we belong to their army. I will start asking questions as we overtake people who look like they might be willing to talk.

"If I hear what I expect to hear, I will give the word and we will launch a surprise attack to try to damage them. But here is the important thing for each of you to remember—there is to be no fighting or causing anyone to worry about us until I give the order. To the contrary, you are to pretend we are part of the army. So you must smile and get along with everyone until I say otherwise.

"If anyone asks, pretend to be stupid; tell them you are one of the newly arrived archers from London and are trying to find out where the army is taking you and who is leading it. Only when I give the order are you to start attacking them. And when I do give it, you are to leave anyone who is unarmed alone and concentrate on killing those who are armed and, in particular, killing or wounding the draught horses and oxen pulling their supply wagons so they cannot be used.

"Cut the throats or bellies of the horses and oxen with your knives or stab them in their guts with the wooden spears we made. And whenever you see sacks or jugs of corn, cut them open with your knives or break them with your stone hammers. We are going to starve the bastards so their arms get weak and sickly and they want to go home."

My men listened carefully and nodded. They had heard it before when I had them begin making their wooden spears and stone hammers. I could see that they understood, so I continued because I wanted them to know that every man was important and no one would be forgotten.

"Hopefully, David and Rolph across the way will see us when we ride down to get on the road and come to join us. We are going to need every man we can get. If they do not join us this morning, we will have to come back and get them later when we return for our supply horses."

******

We were as ready as we could be when I ordered my men to mount up and began leading them in a single file down to the road. A couple of the men were leading our extra horses for use as remounts if they were needed. I had waited until this morning to get started because it had taken all the rest of yesterday for the barons' army and its long baggage train of wains and camp followers to finish passing on the road below us.

The good news was that there never was any sign of the king or a contingent of the king's men, at least not so far as I could see. The bad news was that the pile of stones was quite high—over nine hundred riders and three or four thousand men on foot had passed in front of us.

My two file sergeants had awakened their men before dawn and gotten them fed and ready to mount up and leave. Our supply horses and our tents and the cooking pots were not going with us. They were staying on the hillside because this would likely become one of our permanent camps when we begin attacking the column and trying to cut it off from supplies and reinforcements. Hopefully no one will find them while we are gone.

The sun was just coming up as I led the way through the trees and our gelded rounceys ambled down to the empty road. As we came out of the trees we could see what looked to be a few travellers on the road who might have been stragglers trying to catch up with the column that had passed. We also saw, for the first time in days, people who appeared to be normal travellers and farmers going in both directions.

And there was good news—David and Rolph had been anxiously waiting and watching for us; they came galloping and waving out of the tree line across the way and down to the road as soon as we rode out of the trees. Their arrival brought the number of men under my command up to ten, though it would not be ten much longer—when we reached the road I was going to send another messenger to Okehampton confirming the size of the enemy force and the apparent absence of the king and his men.

Alfred, the chosen man who fought with me at the tin mine, volunteered to carry the message despite the danger he would face because there was now a big force of enemy soldiers on the road between us and Okehampton. He would use two of our best horses; one to ride, one as a remount.

His plan was a good one and I instantly approved it—Alfred was going to ride along the road as if he was some kind of messenger or one of the barons' mounted men, and then just ride on past the front of the barons' column and head for Okehampton as soon as it got dark. He did not know it, but I had be talking to my father and Raymond about him being a sergeant if he makes it.

To everyone's great surprise, David and Rolph were not the only ones who joined us when we reached the road. We had barely turned on to the road and begun following the rear of the barons' army when two messengers from Okehampton showed up with a meaningless parchment from Uncle Raymond reporting that nothing was new.

The two messengers were more than a little relieved to see us; they had spent all of the previous day trying to find us after they got past the barons' army. Similar to David and Rolph, they too had been hiding off the road and watching for us. They had recognized our Egyptian tunic gowns even though we had turned them inside out to conceal our stripes; hopefully, no one else will recognize them.

Including me and Alfred, there were now thirteen mounted archers, every one of them one of our elite outriders, moving up the road to catch up with the barons' army.

******

I led the way and we rode easy along the road for almost an hour until we began to overtake the wains and camp followers at the very end of the barons' long baggage train. Our longbows were strung but over our shoulders as we began casually walking and ambling our horses past wains full of supplies, tents, and even women. As we did, merchants and women began calling out to offer their services and products. We answered with smiles and waves and an occasional "maybe later, luv."

We encountered what we were looking for almost immediately. An older woman was driving a wain filled with girls and women who waved and smiled as we approached. She had temporarily pulled out of the slowly moving baggage train so a couple of her girls could get out of the wain to piss or shite by the side of the road. The girls were adjusting their ragged gowns and coming back to the wain as I pulled up my horse and stopped to talk.

I motioned for my men to continue on past me and gave the woman a friendly wave and smile, and the most bewildered and stupid look I could muster on my face. *This one would know if anyone would.*

"Hoy, missus, and a good day to you, and would you be knowing where we are and what we are doing here? We are the company of archers from London and just arrived. No one tells us much, do they?"

The doxy mother was most friendly and forthcoming and willing to talk. She and her girls were following the army to Cornwall, she said. There was talk of treasure there and she and her girls had come from London in hopes that the men would be kind to her girls and share some of it with them.

I thanked her most kindly with a big smile and said I was sure I would be seeing her again as soon as we got paid the coins we had been promised. Then I kicked my horse in the ribs and moved ahead to catch up to my men who were walking their horses in a single file alongside the barons' baggage train.

We continued slowly passing the camp followers until I reached a poor fellow with a pained look on his sweating face. He was laid out on top of a loaded wain with a following horse tied to it, a poor knight from the look of the battered armour and shield laying near him, and poxed for sure. I held my horse down to match the wain's slow speed and, after a while, began casually chatting him up most friendly.

"Hoy, Sir Knight. When do you think we will get there?" I asked with a most innocent and conversational tone to my voice and a gesture towards the column stretched out in front of us.

His accent when he answered marked him as a Kentish man just like my father and uncle. He was anxious to talk, probably because it distracted him from his sad state.

What he told me in the conversation that followed confirmed what I had heard from the doxy mother and more—his baron and the other barons had reached an agreement with King John; the king had agreed to reinstate their powers and authorities in exchange for some of the religious relics known to be in Cornwall. *Oh Shite.*

Chapter Eight

A different kind of war.

We continued peacefully riding with the barons' baggage train, and slowly passed the people and wains travelling in it, until we came in sight of the first of the many disorganized mobs of soldiers walking behind their baron's mounted men.

No one questioned us or paid us any mind at all. We were just another small group of fighting men among many others. It probably helped that wherever possible we got off the road so no one could talk to us and rode our horses in the fields and pastures that ran alongside of it.

Our horses were particularly good even though some of them were not much to look at until you saw them move—every one of them was a rouncey, bred for the easy gait of an ambler and the speed and stamina required by outriders. And they were trained for use by horse archers and cared for most nicely.

It took several hours because we were riding our horses in an effort not to attract attention, but we finally reached the front of the baggage train and could see the many separate little armies of the barons and their retainers riding and walking in front of us. This was as far forward as most of us would go. Only Alfred and the already-saddled remount he was leading would continue forward and attempt to ride past the barons and their men. If he made it, he would take the verbal message I had given him to the horse archers' base at Okehampton.

"Safe travel, Alfred." I said as we leaned towards each other from our saddles to shake hands. And then for some reason I pulled my little wooden cross out of my tunic and waved it at him.

"We will be praying for you—but do not rely on our prayers; be careful and act innocent. If anyone asks who you are or where you are going, act stupid and distracted and say you are looking for Sir Guy because you have a message for him from his wife about the black pox in the village, and then cough and wipe your brow and do your best to look poxed yourself so they would not want you near them—and, if you can, get close to the head of the column and make your move after everyone scatters to set up their camp for the night and it is too dark for anyone to see you go."

Alfred nodded without saying a word, probably because it was the third time he would heard my orders, and kicked his horse in the ribs to move ahead; I pulled on my reins to slow my horse down so the baggage train with its creaking and squeaking wheels would once again flow past me—and watched him go.

Like the rest of us, Alfred was wearing his archers' tunic gown turned inside out in case any of the barons' men knew about the archers of Cornwall and the stripes which show our ranks.

******

All that morning my archers and I continued peacefully riding near the head of the column in little groups of two or three men. That continued until I saw what I was looking for in the distance in front of me— the road went up a hill so that we on the road on this side of the hill could not see the riders and marching men once they reached the top of the hill and started down the other side. Not being able to see the riders and men in front of us was important because it also meant that the mounted men and their soldiers ahead of us would not be able to look back and see their baggage wains and camp followers when we started attacking them.

I immediately moved up to almost the front of the baggage train with my men and gave them their orders. Then I waited until the last of the barons' fighting men had reached the top of the hill and passed out of sight as they started down the other side. That was when we began our attack.

So as to not attract attention, I led three of my outriders very slowly and peacefully back down the roads towards a place where, if a wain stopped, it would block the road—because a little stream running across the road had created a marshy bog on either side of it that no wain or walker could cross. I had long ago picked out the wain near the front of the column that I intended to stop and use to block the road.

We walked our horses forward as the wain I had selected approached the little stream. It was an overloaded merchant's horse-pulled wain being driven by a woman with an infant strapped to her chest. Immediately behind her were a number of other wains with no one walking near them.

As the woman's wain reached the little stream flowing over the road, I slid off my horse, grabbed the halter of the old plough horse pulling the wain to bring it to a halt, slid an old corn sack over the horse's eyes so it would not bolt, and cut its throat. Then I held tightly to its halter until the horse fell forward on to its knees, rolled over on its side, and died to block the road.

The wide-eyed woman leading the wain had started to scream when I grabbed her horse's halter and cut its throat, but she stopped without making a sound when one of my men lifted a warning finger with a stern look on his face and, a moment later, began slowly counting copper coins into the astonished woman's hand from the pouch I had given him.

"It was an accident and that is what you will tell everyone who asks," the outrider kept repeating over and over again as he leaned forward in his saddle and slowly counted the coins into her hand. She watched the growing pile of coins in her hand as if she was under a spell. After a while, as the number of coins rose higher and higher, she began smiling and nodding her head in agreement.

Two of my men remounted their horses and began walking them down the column to explain why everyone had stopped.

"There is been a mishap up ahead. A horse pulling a wain suddenly died and is blocking the road. It will be cut up and cleared in a bit and there is nothing you can do but get in the way. We have been told to keep everyone away until it is finished, so please stay where you are."

The two archers repeated their story over and over again as they slowly walked their horses along the stalled column. Other archers took positions on either side of the stalled wain to keep everyone back.

In the distance I could see the growing gap between the wain we had stopped and the handful of wains and walkers at the head of the baggage train that had already passed the little stream. They were continuing to move forward on the road. In a few minutes, they too would go over the crest of the hill and disappear from sight.

Three of my archers and Andrew, their sergeant, slowly walked their horses along behind the still-moving wains and walkers who had already gotten past the stream where the road was now blocked. It was their job was to follow those who were continuing over the hill, and then gallop down and warn us when the barons' men began coming to rescue the baggage train. They were also to prevent anyone from the stalled portion of the baggage train from reaching the barons to raise the alarm about our attack.

The four archers would wait on the road at the top of the hill for as long as possible. Then they had ride back to re-join us and we had all run for it back to our camp in the trees.

A few curious people with nothing better to do started forward to see what had happened; they were firmly turned away and sent back with reassurances that they were not needed, and would just get in the way of removing a dead horse that was blocking the road.

"It just up and died in its harness did not it?"

At my request, the now-smiling and totally cooperative woman even stood up the driver's bench of her wain and began motioning for the curiosity seekers to stay back. *So far, so good*.

******

I waited until I could see the road was clear all the way to the top of the hill. Then I gave the signal for my men to start destroying the baggage train. We started at the front of the stalled column and moved rapidly down the road cutting the throats and stabbing the bellies of the horses and oxen as we came to them.

If the horses were jumping about such that we could not get to them quickly and safely with our knives, we stabbed them deep into their guts with our wooden spears. When we came to a wain carrying sacks or amphorae of corn and other supplies, one of the archers would leap off his horse and begin cutting them open with his knife or breaking them with his makeshift stone hammer.

As you might imagine, our ferocious and totally unexpected attack instantly began causing great confusion and chaos all along the road.

Awareness that the stalled baggage train was under attack rippled down the column of stalled wains and walkers like a great ocean wave. There was a great commotion as terrified and hysterical men and women were everywhere screaming and running about in an effort to get away. Others were trying to turn their wains around or attempting to escape by driving them off into the fields along the road.

The screams of the dying and injured horses drove many of the horses we had not yet reached into a frenzy. A few of the oxen tried to run after they were stabbed, but many of them just stood there and shook and shuddered until they fell to the ground and died.

My men and I mostly ignored the screaming horses and terrified people and got about our business of killing and injuring the horses and oxen pulling the supply wains and destroying everything we could get our hands on. Those few of their drivers and owners who tried to stop us or interfere were sliced with our knives or shot down on the spot with an arrow.

For the most part, the men and women in the barons' baggage train responded to our attack by shouting and screaming and running away. And, since we were coming from the front of the baggage train, they either ran towards the rear or towards the safety of the trees in the woods to the north. We made no effort to stop or do harm to the people who merely abandoned their wains; we only rode down and shot those who tried to fight back or tried to go for help.

In the end, only one man was able to mount a horse and gallop up the road towards the barons in an effort to sound the alarm. He did not make it. Andrew and one of his archers in our rear guard rode out to cut him off and quickly brought him down.

The beginning of the end of our attack occurred when a handful riders came over the hill towards the baggage train for some reason and saw that it was under attack. Two of them made the mistake of riding forward to see what was happening. They quickly fell to the arrows of Andrew and his men. At least one the riders, however, must have successfully turned back and sounded the alarm.

"Hoy, Sergeant, lookee."

We had mostly finished with the horses and oxen pulling the wains, and were working our way back to destroy more of the supplies in them, when one of my archers sounded the warning. I looked up to see the archers of our rear guard pounding down the road towards us at a full gallop. We knew why almost immediately—less than a minute later mounted men began pouring over the crest of the hill and coming down the road towards us. At first there were only a few, but soon there were many. It was time to go.

"Saddle up lads," I shouted as I jumped out of the wain where I had been busy smashing amphorae filled with corn and swung into my saddle. "We have done all we can."

I never did see the poxed knight or learn what happened to him.

Chapter Nine

Preparing for war.

Another outrider from Raymond had come in to Restormel. He was the second one today and he was carrying an all-to-believable update to the initial warning message Raymond had received from my son—George thinks that a large force of barons and their retainers is almost certainly marching on Cornwall. He says he and his men counted just over twelve hundred knights and mounted men and about three thousand poorly armed men on foot.

According to George, none of the men in the army appear to be mercenaries or archers. Perhaps even more significantly, my son reported that he did not see any sign of the king or William Marshall or any of the king's men. He did not see any French either, for that matter. It was an army of English barons on their way to Cornwall with their knights and village levies.

What does it mean and how will it affect our efforts to sell the relics? And should we fight to hold our place in Cornwall or load the relics on our galleys and run for our fortified post on Cyprus or elsewhere?

My hastily summoned lieutenants and I looked at each other and I could see the answer on their faces without even asking. It was the same as mine. We had not really expected the barons to do a deal with the king and come after the relics, but we have got too much to lose in Cornwall and we are much stronger than the king or anyone else realizes. We will fight.

I immediately sent out the necessary orders for everyone to prepare our four strongholds for sieges and to move our main body of men to where we had long ago decided was the best place to fight if Cornwall was ever invaded—the River Tamar ford near Lauceston Castle on the border between Cornwall and Devon. I did not even bother trying to recall the archers serving outside of Cornwall; they could not possibly get here in time to participate.

Even worse, we were somewhat unready because we had been spending much of our time trying organize the sale of the relics in order to relieve various and sundry would-be kings and emperors of their coins. Men were shouting and scurrying about everywhere, wains were being loaded, and messengers were constantly coming and going.

I was told to resume my position as Captain William's deputy and chosen man. Henry will command our main army of archers on the Tamar, Raymond will command our horse archers and use them to inflict a constant stream of dangers and privations upon the barons in the Saracen way. And Thomas will take off his mitre and put on his lieutenant's tunic gown to look after our supplies and siege stores. *Poor Thomas, he just sighed and mumbled something about missing his boys and hoping Yoram comes from Cyprus to take over his duties.*

The Tamar ford near Launceston Castle was where the road comes into Cornwall from Exeter and London. There was no doubt about it, the ford was by far the most likely route for the barons' army to travel, and a particularly good place for us to mobilize our forces. We can use the nearby castle as a supply base and as a refuge for our wounded men.

We have fought at the ford before and know it well—it is where we defeated Lord Cornell and ended up with his Hathersage Castle and lands in Derbyshire, and then traded them to the Templars for the horses we needed in order to expand our squadron of horse archers. Indeed, it was nearby at Launceston where I came to Captain William's attention and got the promotion that changed my life so greatly that I now have a wife and my own room in one of the turrets in Restormel's inner wall.

****** *Lieutenant Raymond.*

I started getting ready for war even before the order came in from the captain. George's increasingly alarming reports had been coming into Okehampton and I, of course, had been saddling up fresh couriers and quickly sending his reports on to William at Restormel.

It was clear to me what the reports meant, so I did not wait until William gave his orders; I immediately began getting my men and Okehampton ready for the war and the siege that seems about to be forced on us. Actually, I am looking forward to it. My wife thinks it will give me a good chance to show what my horse archers and I can do.

On the other hand, I am certainly not taking the barons and their men for granted. I have sent word to move our horse herd deep into Cornwall and I have been bringing in more siege supplies and preparing my horse archers to move out on a moment's notice to begin harrying the barons' army. My outriders, of course, are already in place and have commenced harrying the invaders.

I was not worried about the outcome of the coming war despite the fact that we had be outnumbered. Both my horse archers and the company's foot archers use a different and much better way of fighting than the English barons and their poorly trained and equipped village levies. My horse archers and outriders are trained to fight like the Saracens with their constant raids and knife prick attacks, not like the barons and knights who treat war as if it is a big tournament and are always trying to call attention to themselves by demonstrating their individual bravery and ability.

Our company's foot archers are similarly different when they fight on land; they fight and move about together instead of each man for himself. They also carry additional weapons such as three long-handled, bladed pikes for every file of seven archers in addition to short stabbing swords, arrow shields, sharpened stakes, and caltrops.

Thomas says that the way our foot archers fight and march together is the way the old Romans used to fight. I do not know about that, but I have seen for myself that the way William and Henry have our foot archers fight is damn sure more effective than every man fighting an individual enemy, which is how the knights and barons fight.

I am also not worried about my wife being in Okehampton during the war. I have got the castle in good shape for the siege that looks to be coming. We are bringing some of our able-bodied villagers and castle servants in to help man its walls, and sending all the rest of them, and all the women and children away to west to the safety of Trematon and the countryside around it. Those who come in for the siege will live in the stables and in the archers' vacated hovels along the wall in the outer bailey. My wife and Lady Courtney have been most helpful in getting them settled and fed.

I will be away with my men, of course, but I would not be leaving my Wanda and Lady Courtney and her son here unless I was sure they had be safe. And they will be; Okehampton's got its own water well and a huge store of siege food and firewood for cooking, and we are bringing in even more.

We already had enough siege supplies on hand to last for more than a year, but a castle can never have enough when a siege is coming, can it?

****** *Lieutenant Henry*

There was much excitement and activity at our training camp on the Fowey. Everywhere sergeants were shouting, tents were being struck and wains loaded, and galley companies were forming up and getting ready to march. In the distance I could hear the boom of a rowing drum as the archers of yet another galley company set out for Launceston and a place in our rapidly forming army.

By this time tomorrow, our training camp should be almost empty. We were leaving no one behind except a handful of castle defenders in order to put the strongest possible force into the field against the barons. All of our archers and archer apprentices were going to march with our army to Launceston.

Some of the able-bodied construction workers and galley wrights, one or two for every seven-man file of archers, were going as well. They had be assigned to a specific file to carry its water skins and bring bales of arrows forward to its archers when the fighting starts. Others will move into Restormel to help man the walls if it comes under siege. *God forbid that it does, for it would only happen if our army is defeated.* The handful of men who, for one reason or another, were not fit enough to fight or help the fighters would walk or be carried northwest with the women and children to distant Trematon.

I had been busy all morning assigning apprentice archers to their new galley companies and getting the galley companies organized and on their way marching to Launceston. About half of the apprentice archers have been given an early stripe and sent to join their galley companies as qualified archers; the other half have been assigned to their companies as apprentices to further their training.

Restormel was where I had lived ever since my wife and I returned to England when the archers' victory at Harfleur made it too dangerous for me to stay in France. Truth be told, I was happy to return; I liked being a lieutenant in command of the company's archers when they fight on land more than I enjoyed pouring wine for drunken sailors in the south of France. Restormel Castle, of course, was more than just where our company trains its apprentices; it was where our company's captain lived when he was in England, and where my wife and I had our own fine room in one of the turrets of the inner curtain wall.

****** *Lieutenant Thomas*

It was a hectic day. I put on my archer's tunic gown when I awoke and spent all morning organizing convoys of wains to carry siege food to both Okehampton and Launceton and to our war camp in the big pasture next to Launceston Castle.

When I finally got a few minutes of time, I put my bishop's robe and mitre back on long enough to ordain the four oldest boys in my school, and then turned them over to Henry so he could send them out with the archers to be apprentice sergeants and scribes for his senior sergeants.

My assistant, Master Priestly, stayed at Restormel and continued to put the learning on the younger boys whilst I was gone. They were sent off with women and children; if worst came to worst, they would help man the castle's walls.

Most of the archers' wives were sent to Trematon. We moved the rest of them, those who could not go to Trematon for some reason or another, into the castle's outer bailey to keep them safe.

It was surprising how many of the veteran archers have found women. It is probably why they volunteered to stay in Cornwall to help train the apprentices instead of going east in pursuit of prize money. I thought there would be enough siege food and firewood in the castle to keep everyone alive for at least a year and a half. If I had not thought that, I would have culled out more of the women and children and sent them to Trematon.

At the moment I was watching our cattle and sheep boys as they got ready to drive some of our sheep and cattle to Launceston to help feed our army, and the rest to Trematon to feed our refugees. The boys and the two semi-retired archers in charge of them seemed to know what they were doing. I say that because, also at that moment, I was watching with growing dismay as stringers of squawking chickens were being tied together and thrown into a wain on top of each other in a great and twisting mass of flapping wings. All the noise and movement was making the wain horse nervous. Feathers were flying everywhere.

Chapter Ten

The fighting begins.

My outriders and I finally got back to our camp long after the sun had finished passing over England on its daily journey around the world. We had galloped away from the barons' baggage train with joyous whoops and shouts. Our joy did not last for very long.

By the time we found our camp in the dark, I was so stiff and tired I was barely able to dismount. And when I did, I staggered and had to sit down before I could unsaddle my horse and get some water and pour some oats into my cap for him. It was all I could do to take a much needed shite and crawl into one of the tents to get out of the rain. I had never been so tired in my entire life.

Traffic on the road was quite heavy the next morning what with both the road's usual travellers and those coming to and from the barons' army. We began by catching two couriers carrying messages to the barons' army. They contained nothing of importance that needed to be reported to Okehampton, just news from home for a couple of knights being carried by boys from their villages. One poor sod's young son just up and died all sudden like; the other lad we caught was carrying a meaningless message about someone's crops.

We took the boys' horses and sent them back home with a warning that the barons and all their men were doomed, and so were they if we ever saw them again.

A couple of hours later we caught and gave the same warning to a couple of London merchants travelling with horse-drawn wains full of corn and clothes they had hoped to sell to the barons' army, and to a man leading a donkey loaded with the religious charms and garlic cloves needed to ward off various poxes. We sent them all walking back the way they came and kept their horses, wains, and cargos as prizes of war.

One of the merchants' horses looked like it might be quite useful, and my men and I all promptly began carrying some of the charms and garlic cloves in our belt pouches. We let the pedlar keep his donkey and did not bother the local farmers as they went to and from their fields. I immediately decided to kill the merchants' other horse and eat it if we run short of food.

Things got real interesting about the time the sun came out from behind the clouds and was directly overhead. There were eight of us sitting most comfortable in the field at the edge of the trees on the gently sloping hill overlooking the London road.

We were off our horses and eating because old Josh from Crawley had just ridden down from our camp with a sack of fresh flatbread and a cheese for us to carve off pieces with our knives. The field must have been planted two or three weeks earlier because our hobbled horses had their heads down and were quietly feeding on the newly emerging stems of fresh corn.

"Well looky here," Freddy said suddenly as he stood up and pointed up the road towards Cornwall and Devon. His eyes must be tolerably good for all I could see was a smudge of dark on the road where there had not been one before. We all stood up to look.

"What do you see, Freddy?" Sergeant George asked as he held his hand up to shield his eyes from the sun above us and leaned his head forward for a better look.

"Riders coming this way, sergeant. Cannot tell how many there are, can I? But a gaggle of 'em for sure. Seen a glint from a blade, did not I?"

"Check your saddles, lads," our new sergeant said most promptly. But do not mount up or string your bows until I give the word. Josh, you ride back to the camp with the empty food sack and fetch the rest of the lads. Tell them that it looks like a company of horsemen are coming towards us from the barons' army."

"Aye sergeant. I am to fetch the rest of the lads and tell them that it looks like a company of horsemen are coming towards us from the barons' army."

Of course that was what Josh said to the sergeant; one of the first things an archer is learnt is to repeat back any order he is given to make sure he has it true.

****** *George*

We stayed on the hill standing next to our horses and watched as the riders coming down the road towards us got closer and closer. The men from our camp had joined us. Everyone was quite excited and trying not to show it.

"Looks to be at least two or three files of them," someone said quietly as the riders got closer and we could begin to make out individual shapes. "Maybe more."

"A lot more," said someone else with excitement in his voice.

"String your bows, lads; string your bows." I gave the order as I pushed the end of my longbow on the ground to bend it and slip on the bowstring. "We will be using longs."

A few seconds later, I shouted "mount up," and swung into my saddle. I had picked up an extra quiver of arrows before I left camp and now had four; three of them were full of "longs."

We ambled down the hill on our horses and waited in the pasture land running up from the road.

******

My men and I sat there on our horses and waited and watched as the riders came closer. We could see that there were almost thirty of them, heavily armed for sure. The sun periodically raised a flash when it glinted off their armour or blades.

It was a party of knights and no mistake. And they had seen us. They turned off the distant road and began trotting across the pasture towards us. Some of them had already pulled their swords, and those in front lowered their lances even though they were still quite some distance away. They were getting ready for their kind of battle.

I gave the word and nine of us dismounted and handed our reins to the three men I had ordered to act as our horse holders. I did not know for absolute sure, of course, but the party of knights riding towards us was almost certainly sent out to find us and avenge what we had done to the barons' baggage train.

The knights were still trotting across the field towards us when they got within range of our longbows. As they approached what I thought might be the maximum distance our "longs" could fly, I called "up bows" and, a moment later when the knights reached it, I began loudly repeating the command to "push and continue."

Nine strong and experienced archers standing ready with longbows can send their longs quite a distance, and that was exactly what we did. And we did it over and over again so rapidly that there were always arrows in the air as my grunting archers and I held our bowstring to our chests and pushed out our bows with a grunt to set them flying with maximum distance and power. That was immediately followed by a slapping sound as our bowstrings smacked our leather wrist protectors.

I did not count how many arrows I had pushed at the approaching knights before they got close enough for me to shout out "mount up" and swing myself onto my horse, probably five or six. My archers did as well and, being quite experienced and well trained, some or all of them probably pushed out even more.

The results were more than a little encouraging. Only about half of the knights were in the party of charging men that got close enough to make us mount up and ride away. The others were strung out behind them on the ground or trying to help those who were down. And, of those trying to help their wounded friends, almost all of their horses had fallen or bolted. Those who were not still chasing after us were mostly on the ground with arrows in them or on foot because we had hit their horses.

It was no surprise that so many of the knights and their horses had been hit and left behind. The knights may have been wearing helmets and chain and riding horses with armoured chest protectors to turn away an enemy's lance, but that still left other parts of their bodies and their horses for our arrows to find.

Whoever was leading the knights obviously had no experience facing archers with longbows, or they would not have led them into our killing ground without, at least, preparing to receive our arrows.

It was immediately clear from the resulting confusion that the knights had not expected us to start shooting so soon, or at such a distance, or with such accuracy. Many of them did not even have time to drop their helmet visors and raise their shields before our storm of arrows began falling on them. Even so, if the past was any guide, more of the knights went down and broke their bones when their wounded horses bolted or fell than were shot off their horses by taking an arrow. *Either way works quite nicely so far as I am concerned.*

The horses of the knights lumbering in pursuit of us might have been bigger than ours, but ours were faster, and theirs had been ridden harder that morning and their armour-wearing riders were heavier. Little wonder then, that we had little trouble staying ahead of our pursuers and shooting arrows back over our shoulders as we galloped across the fields with the knights strung out behind us in hot pursuit.

One of our pursuers went down almost immediately and, a few minutes thereafter, a second. That was when our pursuers began pulling up their horses and turning back.

From the knights' perspective as they turned back, the battle was over and they had won it by chasing us away. Not from ours; we saw the fighting as we had been learnt to see it—as just beginning.

"Make the turn," I shouted and my two file sergeants quickly echoed. They had been expecting the order as soon as they saw the last knight begin reining in his galloping horse to turn it around and ride back to towards his friends.

Our horses were all high-quality amblers and they were all in good shape. They had barely broken a light sweat by the time I turned my horse to face the retreating knights. My men rode up to gather around me and get their orders.

"Gerard," I shouted as I pointed to where I wanted the sergeant to go, "you take the men from your file and ride way over there to the other side of the road. Chase them from there. Kill them all; you know what you are to do."

"Aye sergeant," he repeated most proper-like, "I am to take my men to the other side of the road and we will do what needs to be done, that we will."

As Gerard and his men galloped off towards the road, I raised my arm and motioned for the men remaining with me, all six of them, to join me in going after our now-retreating pursuers.

The seven of us spread out into a loose line abreast and began cantering, and then galloping, after the retreating knights. Gerard and his men soon crossed the road and began doing the same. We had gone from being the pursued to being the pursuers.

My men and I, and those of Gerard, spread out even more than when we were being chased and shooting backwards over our shoulders. Spreading out is what horse archers with longbows must do when they are pushing out arrows towards targets in front of them.

Due to the great length of our bows, pushing arrows out at targets in front of us requires each archer to hold his bow flat so it protrudes out on either side of his horse. Since we were now riding behind the retreating knights and chasing them, we were holding our bows flat and riding with enough distance between our horses so that the tip of each archer's bow would not interfere with another archer's bow or horse.

According to what we had been learnt in Uncle Thomas's school, pushing arrows from a longbow while riding is inconvenient compared to the ease of using the short bows fancied by the Saracens. Their bows are so short they can be held any which way by a mounted archer without interfering with his mates—but the greater range and power of our longbows more than makes up for the inconvenience caused by their length. At least that was what we had always been told.

The gap between the twelve of us and the closest of the knights who had turned back got smaller and smaller even though they saw us coming after them and whipped up their horses. Our horses were fresher, faster, and less burdened. We began to catch up to them one at a time, their thrusters first.

Because he was the last of our pursuers to turn around, the first of our pursuers to fall was the thruster who had ridden ahead of his friends and come closest to catching us. He was lightly bearded, armoured only with a helmet and a chain shirt, and riding a slightly smaller horse than the others. Probably an ambitious squire seeking his spurs or a newly made and overly excited young knight trying to impress his friends.

There was a solid "thunk" as an armour piercing heavy from one of my men slammed into the knight's back. He flinched and continued kicking his horse in the ribs in an effort to get away. That lasted until one of my men rode closer and hit him again with an arrow higher up on his back.

He slowly slid sideways out of his saddle and rolled head over heels in a somersault until he came down to a rest on his back. His horse kept running.

"Damn it. The bastard broke my arrow for sure" was the only comment I heard from my men as I slowed down to see if the fallen rider needed a third. He did not, so I kicked my horse in the ribs and hurried to catch up to my men.

The knight galloping in front of the fallen thruster had seen his friend's fate. A few seconds later, he stopped trying to gallop his horse straight back to join the others. He tried, instead, to turn hard to the right to get away from our line of advance. It was a mistake.

Turning his horse broadside to us presented us with a wonderful target. Four or five of my men immediately pushed arrows at him and at least two, and possibly three, slammed into the side of his horse. It went down and rolled over him. I did not even slow down to make sure he was finished; neither did any of my men.

One after another, similar fates befell the rest of the riders who had once been our pursuers. In the end, only seven or eight of our pursuers, those who had turned back the earliest, reached our original killing grounds and the knights who had stopped there for one reason or another.

The wounded knights and those who were off their horses were waiting and watching as the first of the riders we were chasing began to reach them. They had not realized, at first, that the returning pursuers were themselves now being pursued. They probably thought that my men and I coming in behind the fleeing knights were more of their own party who were returning after successfully driving us away.

Everything changed when the first of the now-desperate returnees got close to the wounded knights and those who had been unhorsed or had dismounted to be with their dead and wounded friends. That was when they finally understood what was happening.

At first, some of them began readying themselves to stand there and fight us. They drew their swords and raised their shields. They were mostly the lightly wounded and the friends and relatives who had stayed behind to assist the seriously wounded and give mercies to those who could not be saved or were suffering great agonies.

In the distance beyond the waiting knights, I could see Gerard and his men arriving at the place on the other side of the road where I had told them to position themselves. We were no longer outnumbered.

******

Everything had changed by the time we got within arrow range of the knights who had stayed behind with their wounded friends. Every one of them who could had either mounted his horse or was attempting to mount it.

Now there were a dozen or more knights on horseback and three or four on foot out of the original party of thirty or so who had tried to attack us. Several of those on foot were desperately trying to mount their excited horses, and finding it difficult because there was no one to help them and they were heavily burdened with armour and weapons.

"Longs," I shouted as I pushed an arrow towards one of the mounted knights. "Break them up with longs." One of my quivers was already empty and another was only half full. It was a good thing I had decided to carry a fourth.

My men and I began to send a steady stream of arrows into the men and horses we were rapidly approaching. They promptly raised their shields and dropped their visors. A horse was hit and bolted almost immediately and threw his rider, and then a man was hit, and then two more horses were hit almost at the same moment.

Suddenly the knights who were still mounted broke and abandoned those who had been unhorsed—first one, and then all of them galloped for the road and headed west towards the safety of the barons' army. Three or four wounded men were moving on the ground or trying to stand up. From the looks of their gestures, they were beseeching the mounted men not to abandon them.

We gave a wide berth to the unhorsed men and galloped after the knights trying to escape. So did Gerard and his men on the other side of the road. We had come back later to pick up the armour and weapons of those who could not flee.

All semblance of order deserted the fleeing knights. It was every man for himself as we galloped behind them and on either side of the road alongside of them—and constantly pushed arrows at them whenever we had a shot.

One after another the fleeing men went down, usually when their horse took an arrow in its rump.

I had only been a little tyke when my father was fighting the Saracens but now, really for the first time, I understood why the Saracens had been so successful in preventing reinforcements and pilgrims from reaching Jerusalem despite the efforts of the Templars and Hospitallers to fight them off—because the Saracens rode their horses as we were riding ours, to stay away from the knights' swords and lances and keep shooting arrows at them until either the knights or their horses went down.

******

The horse of the last knight went down after we chased him into a wooded area far off the road. Gerard pushed out an absolutely splendid shot as the horse was being ridden through a clump of trees and hit it squarely in the side. It bolted forward another twenty lengths or so, bounced off a tree, and fell over trapping its rider beneath it.

Two of my outriders and I rode up all out of breath. We pulled up our horses and watched as a young knight struggled to get himself out from under the fallen and still struggling horse. He stopped trying and just looked at us when we reached him. I raised my hand and motioned for my men not to shoot.

"Do not move," I gasped as I pulled my exhausted horse to a halt about ten feet away from the battered and equally exhausted knight and pointed an arrow at him. He stopped trying to pull his leg out from under the horse and made the sign of the cross. There was a look of despair in his eyes; he knew he was about to die.

It had been a hard and long ride for me, but he was the last of them and I, at least, would be riding away from here alive.

"Can you pull yourself free?" I finally asked, and then motioned with my hand that he should go ahead and try.

"Aye, I think so," the young man answered. He had a Yorkish accent. He was a poor knight from the look of his armour and quite young. His horse gave a last big lurch and began pissing and trembling as it finished its dying and the knight's leg somehow came out.

"Stand up and take off your armour," I ordered him.

He had to struggle to get to his feet because of the weight of his armour, and I could see him look about and test his legs as he did. It was instantly clear that he was going to try to make a "forlorn hope," a desperate run to escape.

"Do not even think about it," I said with a shake of my head as I pushed my bow out towards him.

"I saw you make the sign of the cross. Do you want to die so soon?"

* * * * * *

I thought of the despair in the eyes of the young knight whose armour, sword, and saddle Gerard was now carrying as we walked our tired horses out from under the cover of the trees and into the light rain that had begun to fall. It was time to retrace our steps, finish off the unhorsed knights who still needed to be finished off, and gather up the weapons and armour of those who had come to attack us. My bones and arse ached.

Each of the knights we find alive will get the same choice as the man Gerard and I left in the forest—either die here and now with an arrow in your belly, or swear a knightly oath to the Pope that you will return straight to your home, always assist the archers and people of Cornwall whenever they need it, and never again take up arms against them or aid anyone who would do them harm.

If you break your oath, I had warned the young knight before he gave it, "you will stay in purgatory forever because the archers and the men of Cornwall have God and the Pope on their side." *I was not at all sure of that, but it sounded fearsome when I said it and my men were impressed.*

"Besides that," I had added, "either the Pope or the Bishop of Cornwall will almost certainly hear from a priest about your breaking of your oath, and send someone to find you and kill you most foul."

Now there is an idea. Uncle Thomas made much about the Arab assassins when he was putting the learning us; I wonder if there are any in England we could employ?

Chapter Eleven

The horse archers get ready.

Their women and the castle defenders who would be staying behind watched intently and waved and cried out as almost one hundred and seventy horse archers and their heavily loaded supply horses clattered out over Okehampton's two drawbridges. Lieutenant Raymond was leading the way on his black gelding. Some of the horse archers' wives and children ran after them; others just stood and watched them go and either wept and clutched their children tightly or talked quietly among themselves.

The horse archers were going to war and it would be the first real war that the young ones among them had ever experienced. Most of them were excited and more than a few were worried and trying not to show it. More would have been worried if they had known their lieutenant was determined to seek out the barons' army and do much more than just harass and weaken it as Captain William and his other lieutenants expected. It was his wife's idea.

There was more than a little good thinking in Lieutenant Raymond's intentions and his wife's idea that he and his men should try to destroy the barons' army before it even got to Cornwall. His archers were trained to fight both as mounted archers as the outriders fight, and as fast-moving heavy infantry with the larger shield, short sword, bladed pike, caltrops, and two sharpened stakes that each archer's supply horse carries in addition to a rain skin and food for the archer and his two horses.

No one had ever before had troops who were trained and equipped with the most modern of weapons to fight both on foot and on horses, not in England or anywhere else, not even the Romans. The barons and knights fought more like the barbarians and Scots where every man fought by himself for glory and recognition, even when they stood side by side in a shield wall or charged forward in groups. Individually is how the barons and knights usually fought—and they had never come up against trained and organized men armed with longbows or hooked pikes with very long handles.

****** *Lieutenant Raymond*

Okehampton's two drawbridges creaked and clanked as they were raised behind us. They would not come down until we return, except momentarily to let a messenger enter, and never at the same time. The senior sergeant in command of the castle and his number two are both dependable veterans with wives and children in the castle. I know them well and I am confident they will see to it that the castle is properly defended, if only because of their families. *They also know that if they do not do everything possible to defend it, and particularly if they let themselves be gulled into letting the enemy enter, they will lose their stripes and I will hang them.*

I led my men out of the castle and almost immediately turned off the cart path and headed north across the castle's fields and pastures. My men had no idea where I was leading them. Even Francis, a senior sergeant with five stripes and my second in command, did not know.

None of my men knew where our war camp would be located because I wanted to keep it a secret for as long as possible. Captain William and my three fellow lieutenants know where it is, of course, because I had showed them on the leather map I taken with me to the meeting at Restormel. The only other person who knew was Wanda, my dear wife from the land on the other side of the Saracen's desert. She should; it was her idea.

It took almost the entire day for my men and me to ride to the campsite I had long ago chosen in this part of Devon. It was north of the road to Cornwall and in an isolated corner of the Okehampton land now owned by William as the earl of Cornwall. It was on a tree-covered hill a good day's walk from Okehampton and Launceston, and deliberately far away so we had have plenty of time to get ready in case the army besieging the castle got tired of our many little attacks and decided to end their siege and come for us instead.

I chose the place because of how long it would take an army with men on foot to walk to it from the London road, and because it has good view of the surrounding countryside and a little stream running through it where we can water our horses and men. From here, if we did not run into trouble and have to fight or detour, we would be able to reach both Okehampton and Launceston in half a day of steady riding.

****** *Senior Sergeant Francis*

It was a busy time for me as Raymond's number two. Every four-stripe company sergeant and his three-stripe file sergeants wanted his men and horses near the stream so as to be close to the water. I was not having that, of course, and made them move. *Lieutenant Thomas might show up and find a man or his horse pissing or dropping a turd in the water; I am not risking my stripes for that.*

We stayed on the hill where Lieutenant Raymond had led us several days ago until Kenneth, the tinker's son from York, rode in from watching Okehampton to report that the first of the barons' army had reached the castle and been denied entry when they asked for hospitality for the night. I knew all about it because we had gathered around the cooking fire that night and talked to Kenneth Tinker ourselves after he reported to the Lieutenant.

Kenneth told us the barons appeared to be setting up what looked to be a siege camp where the cart path to Okehampton Castle turns off from where the London road bends to go south towards Exeter.

That the barons would assemble their army in front of Okehampton was to be expected. It was the best place for the barons coming from the north and from London to join up with the men the Earl of Devon would be bringing up from Exeter.

What really surprised all of us, however, was when Kenneth said how pleased Raymond seemed to be when he heard the news. I would have thought he would have been concerned, what with his wife in the castle and such. I certainly was because my wife and two little children were there. I had already lost one family to the sweating pox, I did not want to lose another.

Kenneth told us he had been watching the cart path to the castle from a hide he had built where the little stream runs through the stand of oak trees in the south pasture. He also confirmed what we had already heard from our outriders watching the Exeter road, that the barons' army assembling in front of Okehampton had been joined by a large force of men from Exeter led by the Earl of Devon, some of whom appeared to be wounded. *Wounded? Of course; Michael the mason and his outriders must have caught them on the Exeter road.*

All of our men were talking excitedly and trying to guess what would happen next? Rumours were constantly flying about like a swarm of bitey bugs. Would the barons and Devon remain where they are now camped and lay a siege on the castle, or would they march on Cornwall, or would some of them go and some of them stay?

Everyone had a different opinion and many claimed to have talked to someone who knew for sure all about our enemy's plans. I was curious myself, of course, but it did not really matter; the Lieutenant Raymond had already told us how we had be fighting no matter who our enemies might turn out to be or where they decided to establish their camp or camps.

****** *Lieutenant Raymond*

I drew a circle in the dirt as Francis and my seven four-stripe sergeants stood around me. They were there because they each commanded one of our 21-man horse companies. In the middle of the circle I scratched an "X" and called it the barons' army. Then I assigned each of their companies to a position on the circle I drew around the "X."

My plan was simple and fully understood by each of the seven company sergeants and his three file sergeants. They should have understood it; we had been constantly practicing what we had be doing over and over again for some years.

It was a simple plan. We were going to put a loose circle of mounted longbow archers all the way around the bastards and use the greater range of our "longs" to keep the barons' men in constant danger. We had fall back if they sallied forth, and move back closer when they fell back—and constantly push an arrow at them whenever an archer sees a target. In other words, we had be the bees constantly stinging the bear who was going after our honey. And if the bear moved towards Cornwall or anywhere else, our circle of archers would move with him, and keep stinging and stinging and stinging.

"Remember lads," I said as I finished giving my sergeants their orders and positions. "The important thing is to keep your men constantly trying to kill the bastards and their horses. No man can go wrong if he stays near the enemy and pushes out an arrow whenever he has an opportunity."

Then, after a moment's pause, I added a bit of good news and a warning to go with it.

"Neither George's outriders on the London road nor those of Michael the mason on the Exeter road have reported seeing any Genoese crossbow men. And the barons have not ever had very many archers in their own ranks in the past, have they? But that do not mean there would not be some among them, does it? So tell your lads to be careful and remind them that it takes a crossbow man a long time to reload a new quarrel.

"Also remind them to pick up their arrows whenever possible and reuse them. We have got bales and bales of extra arrows as we all know, but an archer can never have enough, can he?"

******

I finished giving orders to my sergeants and we rode out of our war camp less than an hour after Kenneth reported that the barons' army was gathering near the Okehampton cart path, and looked to be settling in for a siege. I could only hope the news is true—it is time for the barons to be learnt that only a fool attacks Cornwall's lands and our company of archers. And I have got just the men to do it—seven full horse companies mounted on strong rouncey amblers, and each company with a company sergeant and three seven-man files under a three-stripe file sergeant.

All in all, that was one hundred and fifty-six men going out to fight as horse archers counting me and the young man Thomas sent to me to gobble church-talk when someone dies and fetch for me as my scribe. He is a three-stripe apprentice sergeant just like George, Captain William's son, was before he earned his fourth stripe.

I led the horse archers out of the camp riding at the head of my Number One Company, the company I myself would be leading into the fighting that was sure to begin as early as tomorrow. What the barons did not yet know, and my men and my new young scribe did not yet fully realize, was that the fighting was going to continue constantly until either our enemies were gone or we had run out of arrows. Well, they had find out soon enough; yes they would.

All of my men were going out as mounted archers. Accordingly, each man's personal supply horse, and thus his shield, short sword, and pike that his supply horse carries so he can also fight on foot, were left behind in our war camp in case he needed his land fighting weapons later. At the moment he did not. Today every man was going out to fight as a mounted archer and carrying five full quivers of arrows, mostly longs, and a ten days supply of cheese and bread for himself and oats for his horse.

In addition, the men in each seven-man file were leading two supply horses carrying a tent, a hammered breast plate to cook flatbread, and extra bales of longs. We had sleep rough and each company would use its supply horses to carry its wounded back to its camp and fetch more food and arrows. *That was the plan my wife helped me put together; she is very good at thinking behind her eyes.*

We all rode together for a while and then, with shouts of encouragement and good wishes, each horse company went its own way under its four-stripe company sergeant, twenty-two men in every company. Each would each operate independently as part of the circle of horse archers I was placing all around the enemy army.

The assignment I had given to each company sergeant and every archer was simple—get in contact with the enemy and stay in contact. Fall back pushing arrows at them when they advance against you; move forward pushing arrows at them when they fall back. In other words, never let the bastards feel safe and kill them every chance you get until they break and run. Then ride them down and kill them.

Francis stayed behind with a few men to sergeant our war camp whilst I was away leading Number One Horse Company. I had to be out with one of my companies somewhere or my men might think less of me—even if it was much to the displeasure of John from London who was the company's four-stripe sergeant and wanted to lead it himself instead of riding beside me as my number two. Ah well, John's a good man, he is. He will get over it, yes he will.

Number One Company's position on the circle of archers surrounding the enemy army was one of the most important because it would be between Exeter and Okehampton; Exeter being where the barons would likely look to for supplies and might try to run after we defeat them. We would not be totally alone; I had already placed Michael the mason and his two files of outriders astride the Exeter road to harass Devon and his men, and to cut the road totally once Devon and his men came past.

****** *Lieutenant Henry*

Messengers have been coming in constantly from Raymond with news of the barons' army. The latest word is that the barons are assembling their army in a camp along both sides of the cart path leading up to Okehampton Castle. As we expected, they have been joined by the Earl of Devon and his men.

They should have moved faster. All nineteen of our fully equipped foot companies of archers, over fifteen hundred archers with longbows, short swords, shields, and bladed pikes, and another four or five hundred local men and sailors to bring them water and keep them supplied with arrows, were now either already in place at the River Tamar ford or would be there in the next few hours.

William was pleased with our strength and said as much as he and Peter and I stood wolfing down bread and cheese as we watched another foot company of archers and their carriers march down towards its position in the line we were forming on the Cornwall side of the Tamar ford. They were marching on the side of the cart path because the cart path coming up from the ford was packed with the wains and people and livestock we were sending west to escape the fighting that was sure to come.

At the moment, the ford was filled with people and a flock of sheep splashing across in the muddy water. They were on their way to safety deep in Cornwall. Our great horse herd had come through yesterday afternoon, but there was still a mass of people and sheep gathered on the other side waiting to cross. One of our companies was on the Devon side of the river helping to organize them, and another was at the ford helping to bring them across, carrying the babies and the lambs and such.

"If Raymond's outriders have counted proper, the barons have only got about six thousand men including Devon's, and we have got over sixteen hundred archers with longbows and almost nine hundred of them are also carrying bladed pikes. We will destroy the bastards," William growled.

"I know; I know," I replied. "Our line looks strong. But I still want to put another company in reserve behind it. No sense taking chances, eh? Besides, if we place them there, they will be easier to move if the barons try to slip a force across the river somewhere else to get behind us."

What I was concerned about was something that has never yet happened such that William and Peter seem to have stopped worrying about it—a force of enemy knights and their soldiers either breaks through our line or somehow gets around behind us because we do not have enough men in reserve who can be sent to confront them.

It could happen; God forbid, it could happen; our men running because someone breaks into our line or attacks us from behind. We may be as nicely equipped and trained as William thinks, indeed we are; but you never know what surprises an enemy might throw at you, or how your men will react when he does.

I breathed a sigh of relief when William agreed to let me hold another company in reserve, and I promptly gave the necessary orders.

"Hoy there, Freddie. Move your company back from the river to where the cart path bends by the big pile of rocks; you will be the reserve for the right side of our line. I will be wanting you to move fast to attack an enemy breakthrough or to turn sideways and go down the river path if anyone tries to flank us or gets behind us."

Chapter Twelve

The fighting begins.

Number One Company rode south towards the Exeter road for hours with me riding at their head. Both their four-stripe company sergeant, John, the one-time butcher from London, and young Richard, my priestly new sergeant apprentice and scribe riding along side of me. We had ridden out of our war camp with the other companies but they soon began peeling off to head for their assigned positions in the circle of horse archers I was putting around the enemy army.

Within a few hours we were twenty-four men riding alone through the Devon countryside on the east side of the Tamar. It was strangely silent and empty, not at all the way I had seen it in the past when I had ridden this way. No one was working in the fields, and both of the Okehampton villages we passed seemed deserted. Way off on our left we could see one of our companies as it moved across a distant field. There were not any sheep or cattle in the pastures.

The absence of any activity and people was reassuring. The villagers in this part of Devon lived on Okehampton lands, the only lands in Devon owned by Cornwall, and had been ordered to take their families and their sheep and cattle and head for the safety of Cornwall.

******

I had just dismounted to piss and barely lifted my tunic gown and gotten started when everything changed. Out of the corner of my eye I saw one of my archers stand in his saddle and point to the east. I was still shaking my dingle when I turned to look where he was pointing. What I saw in the distance was a line of mounted men following two horse carts, each with a driver and a couple of men riding in it and some men walking beside it. There were ten or eleven riders and they were coming around a hill about a mile ahead of us—and heading straight towards us.

They saw us at the same time we saw them. *A foraging party, by God.*

"John, take your number one file and get around to the north of them; the rest of you, string your bows and follow me," I shouted as I finished shaking my dingle and moved quickly to swing back up into my saddle.

My horse caught my excitement and my sudden move to remount. It jerked its head and pranced sideways a couple of steps as I pulled myself up into the saddle and leaned over to push the tip of my bow against the ground to bend it so I could string it. All around me excited men on excited horses were stringing their bows and pulling arrows out of their quivers.

* * * * * *

At first, the riders from the foraging party trotted forward to meet us. Perhaps to see who we might be; perhaps to attack us because they already knew we were not friendly. It did not matter. I responded by leading my two files of men south instead of straight at them and John led the seven men of his number one file off to the north so as to get on the other side of them.

My men and I rode away to the south so any knights accompanying the party would think we were afraid of them and trying to escape. We wanted them try to catch us, and that was what they did. They galloped after us.

As our pursuers came closer and closer, I could see that some of the riders riding towards us, three or four of them, were knights wearing armour. The others were undoubtedly their squires and mounted retainers and men-at-arms. Despite the distance still separating us, some of our pursuers had already couched their lances and others had drawn their swords.

I had no intention, of course, of meeting them head-on as if this was some kind of tournament in which everyone fought according to the prevailing rules and knightly traditions. To the contrary, my intention was to kill or wound them all and take their weapons and armour; accordingly, I increased my horse's speed slightly and led my men south as if I was trying to avoid a battle. At the same time, John and his men galloped north. As I expected, the knights followed my larger body of riders and ignored John's.

The knights and their mounted men may have thought we were attempting to flee and been greatly heartened by it. They totally abandoned the two horse carts they were escorting and chased after us. It did not work for them. No matter how hard they tried, their horses bred to carry armoured knights with swords, shields, and lances into battle could not catch our horses, every one of them a gelded ambler bred for their easy gait and their speed and stamina.

Our pursuers finally abandoned their pursuit and turned back on their exhausted horses. They turned back too late to save the horse cart and the men they had abandoned. John and his archers had already swooped in and killed them all, including the horses pulling the two-wheeled carts. Now it was the knights' turn.

We immediately pulled our horses around and began to ride after our increasingly desperate one-time pursuers. One after another we caught up to them and shot them down with each of us giving every fallen rider we passed another arrow to keep him down. None of our pursuers or their horses survived.

The rest of the day was spent picking up our arrows and stripping the dead men of their armour and weapons and throwing them into one of the foragers' carts. It was near to getting dark by the time we finished stripping the dead foragers and gathering up everything of value, so we took the cart with us and camped nearby for the night.

******

"Lieutenant, do you think the barons will send out a search party to see what happened to their foragers?"

That was the question John asked me the next morning with a gesture towards the swarms of birds which had begun circling over their bodies scattered about where we had left them. He asked it as we ate some of the bread and cheese we were carrying and got ready to leave the campsite in the trees where we had spent the night.

The men sitting around us heard him ask the question and stopped eating to listen to my answer. Little wonder in that; they knew there would be a bit of prize money if the armour and other valuables we had collected were sold to merchants or bought in by the company for our men to use. They also knew they would not get any prize money if a search party or other foragers found the cart and made off with the valuables before we returned.

"Well, they certainly would not have trouble finding the men we killed," I said with a gesture towards the circling birds and a smile. *I knew what he was really asking.* "But not their valuables; we are going to take them away from here and hide them someplace else."

I said it loud enough so the men could hear.

There was good reason for the men's interest and their nods of satisfaction when they heard my answer. Yesterday afternoon we had collected the weapons, armour, and other valuables from the men we had killed and brought them with us to a camp we hastily established nearby. John and his men were worried that they would lose their prize monies if what they had taken off the dead foragers was found and carried away by someone else.

A few minutes later we mounted up and rode out of the trees. We took the cart full of captured armour and weapons with us and hid it a couple of miles away in a thick stand of trees.

******

John and I led Number One Company south and east all morning until the Exeter road finally came into sight just after the sun passed overhead and began moving west. There was no traffic on the road and that made the whereabouts of the road hard to see in the distance.

At first, because there was no traffic on it, I could not see the road even when the men around me began commenting that they could see it. Finally, I saw the road and we turned towards it in a battle formation with me leading one file, John another, and a file sergeant the third. We rode with two or three hundred paces of distance between each file.

We reached the Exeter road without seeing anyone in the fields or travelling on it. But we were not sure how close we were to Exeter. None of us had ever been this far south into the Earl of Devon's lands.

I rode on the road itself with the men of my file spread out in a line behind me. John and his file rode far out in the field to my left; Jack, a three-stripe file sergeant, rode with his file far out in the fields on the right. We had to keep riding like this until either it got too dark to continue or we made contact with enemy.

Suddenly we came upon several families ploughing and planting a field on Jack's side of the road. These were obviously Devon's lands or they would have been off to Cornwall.

The men and a couple of boys were straining to pull an old fashioned wooden plough with a woman riding on it. Another woman with an infant on her back was walking behind the plough sprinkling seeds. They stopped and looked at us as we approached, but did not run. It was an altogether peaceful scene.

"Hoy," I said with a smile as I walked my horse up to them. *They look tired; I suspect they are pleased to have an excuse to stop.*

"Hoy," was the response, followed by a flood of words coming out of the plough woman's mouth in some strange dialect and much pointing down the road.

"John," I shouted to the company sergeant who was cantering over to us from where he had been riding further off to the left. "Do any of your lads know how to gobble with these people?"

A young archer who had been leading one of the supply horses was called over from the file which had been riding with John in the fields on the left side of the road. He gobbled back and forth with the grey-haired woman on the plough for some time. Some of what he was told was encouraging; some was not of much value.

What the lad learnt was that the plough woman and her family were slaves owned by the Earl of Devon. They had been working in the fields from dawn to dusk ever since the first day of spring ploughing. Several days ago they had seen a "very big" number of men riding horses and walking on the road. They had watched them pass.

The problem was that "very big" could mean hundreds of men or thousands—she did not know how to count, just that there were as many men as onions in three or four sacks.

I reached into the pouch on my belt for a penny and tossed it to the woman with a nod of appreciation. She looked at it in wonder and broke into a big toothless smile. *Have to keep them friendly, do not we? We may be back through here again.*

We remounted our horses and continued moving north towards Okehampton as soon as John's archer finished talking to Devon's slaves. John rode with me on the road and so did Richard, my apprentice sergeant and scribe. As we began to move forward, I noticed the young archer wheel his horse around and walk it and the supply horse he was leading back to say a few more words to the woman and point towards Cornwall. Then he cantered his horses to catch up with his file.

"He is from Devon." John explained quietly when he noticed me watching the archer ride back to join his mates. "He was a slave until his family escaped from Devon to join us in Cornwall."

Chapter Thirteen

We find more foragers

We continued riding until, far off to our left, we saw a couple of horse-drawn wains and a small party of men. They were on a rough cart path and coming towards us from the hovels of one of Devon's villages. Several of them were mounted and riding in front of the wains; the others were walking behind it. What we could not see was whether the men were armed or not.

"Spread further out," I ordered as I motioned with my hand towards the files riding off to both sides of me and led my own file off the road to ride directly towards the distant men.

"But do not push any arrows at them unless I give the order." *They might be peaceful villagers and have useful information.*

I picked up the pace and our horses were soon ambling through a field of corn stalks towards the distant party of men. My archers were now spread out in a long line on either side of me.

******

"Lieutenant, I think they are armed," someone shouted.

A few minutes later I could see for myself. They were armed. It was, as I had expected and hoped, an enemy foraging party, not villagers going home after a hard day of working in the fields. It was similar to the foraging party we destroyed yesterday except there were only a couple of mounted men and they did not make the mistake of chasing after us.

"String your bows," I shouted as I pulled my horse to a stop and leaned over to press the tip of my bow against the ground and string it. The sergeants and chosen men quickly repeated my order and all along our line the archers reined in their horses and strung their bows.

I kicked my horse in the ribs and started it ambling towards the distant wain as soon as I finished getting my bow ready. My men were soon strung out in a long line on either side of me.

We ambled towards the enemy foragers at an easy pace. They had seen us coming and stopped on the cart path to watch us approach. We got quite close before they realized we were not friendly. Perhaps they were misled because we were coming from the direction of Exeter and they thought we were part of their army.

The foragers' lack of concern changed when they saw our nocked arrows and finally realized we were an enemy and had them hopelessly outnumbered; then it was every man for himself. The men on foot abandoned the wains and ran in all directions except for two who managed to jumped into one of the wains as its driver whipped up his horse in an effort to escape; the two horsemen wheeled their horses and attempted to gallop away.

It did not do any of them any good. We killed them all and captured two wains loaded with sacks of corn and the horses pulling them. I decided to keep the wains and horses.

******

Less than an hour after our second one-sided little battle, we resumed our march to get us closer to Okehampton with our newly acquired wains clattering along behind us. They were heavily loaded with the dead men's saddles, weapons, and armour riding on top of the corn sacks. An archer was driving the horse pulling each of the wains with his saddled riding horse tied behind it and ready to be mounted on a moment's notice.

We reached the Exeter road in time to meet a fast-moving galloper on his way to Exeter. He was riding a good horse, but it was tired and he was not leading a remount. Three of the archers caught him after a fairly long chase and killed him and his horse as well. They brought back his particularly fine leather saddle but no parchment for Richard to read to me. We never did find out why he was in such a hurry.

The sun was just finishing passing overhead and the three archers had long ago brought us the courier's saddle when we overtook another foraging party and their wain. They were going slowly because of the rather large herd of sheep they were driving up the road towards their Okehampton camp.

We killed them all, the foragers that is, and took their wain which was loaded with a couple of sacks of corn, a broken loom, and some bowls and bedding. It was so dark by the time we finished collecting their weapons and armour that we may not have gotten it all. It is also possible that a couple of the foragers on foot escaped in the dark into the nearby trees.

I had a couple of the sheep slaughtered whilst the foragers' weapons were being gathered, and had the rest of the flock and the three wains driven into the field next to the road. I thought about killing the sheep and scattering the corn to keep them out of the hands of the barons' men, but I did not order it done because we might need them for ourselves; I decided to wait until morning to make up my mind.

It was dark and cloudy that summer night and it started to rain. We pulled the wains off the road; used flint, pounded iron, and a feather stick to get a fire going so we could burn strips of mutton on the tips of our knives; and slept under the wains with our weapons and saddled horses nearby and four men awake and on guard at all times. It had been another good day even though my lice itched something fierce.

******

My men and I were up and ready to ride before dawn on a damp and cloudy morning. The rain had stopped sometime in the night, and I could see mist rising from the ground as the sun appeared and began another day of endlessly circling the earth. The men on watch had been able to keep the fire going all night under one of the wains, and I awoke to the smell of fresh flatbread and freshly burnt mutton strips.

For some reason I awoke with a question in my head—why had armed foraging parties been going to

Devon's own villages to find food? The corn and sheep, after all, already belonged to Devon; he did not need his men to take them by force. The only possible answer I could think of was that the foragers were armed so they could defend the supplies they were bringing back to their camp. It did not matter. They were dead and we had their corn and sheep. But their being armed meant something and I did not know what it was.

The question vexed me and I could not get it out of my head as I put slices of mutton on my knife and held them into the fire to burn.

Suddenly, as if delivered by God, something came into my head about what it might mean—they were armed because they thought they might have to defend the forage they were collecting. Yes, that was it for sure; they must have known my horse archers and I were out in force. But how would they have known we had be so far south? And if they had known about us, why did not they send more men to guard the foragers? It was all very confusing.

I was still thinking about why the foragers were armed when I finally mounted my horse and we once again began to ride up the road towards the barons' army. We got away late because I had decided we should keep the sheep and the wains full of corn and loot. I had my men drive them over a distant hill and into a stand of trees so they could not be seen from the road. *My men did not know it, of course, but I did not order them to kill the sheep and scatter the corn so we could use it to stay out here on Devon's land and feed ourselves until the barons' army is destroyed.*

Once again I thought about leaving a man to guard the food and weapons we had captured, and once again I did not—so we had have every man if we got into another fight as we almost certainly will. Better to lose the captured food and weapons, I decided, than lose a battle because I did not have enough archers.

William and the lads at Restormel think we are riding to prevent the barons' army from foraging on its way to Cornwall. We are not so far as I am concerned; we are here to totally destroy their army with a thousand little cuts so it dies before it reaches Cornwall. It was my wife's idea. She says that was how her people like to fight. If possible, we will use the captured food in order to stay here and do just that.

******

"Hoy, Lieutenant, riders coming up behind us."

I was shaken out of my thoughts by the shout. I stood in my saddle to look—and recognized them as they came closer. It was Michael the mason from York and his outriders, by God. They must have thought we are foragers and were coming to attack us. Good for them. I stood as I high as could get on my horse and waved.

Bows were lowered and unstrung, and smiles appeared on everyone's faces as Michael and his men pounded up to us and reined in their horses. They were as pleased to see us as we were to see them.

"Hoy, Lieutenant," Michael said with a smile as he reined in next to me. His horse moved about a bit as he did and we both dismounted.

"I did not expect to see you here, Lieutenant, did I?" Michael said with a question in his voice as he knuckled his head and grasped my outstretched hand to shake it. Then he asked, "is all well with you? And do you have any extra food and arrows you can spare? We are almost out, are not we?"

Michael reported what he and his men had done so far and their current state. He and eleven of his original outriders were available to ride with us; one of his men, an archer from a village near Trematon, had been killed and two others had been wounded seriously enough that they could not ride a horse and fight. They were wounded while they were harassing the Earl of

Devon's army as it came up the road to join the barons' army assembling in front of Okehampton.

"We rode along in the fields next to them and loosed arrows at their column for two days, did not we?" he explained. *No wonder Exeter had wounded with him when he joined the barons.*

Michael's two wounded men were in a captured horse cart which had been pulled off the road and temporarily abandoned when they saw us and galloped forward to see if we needed killing.

It is a good thing Michael and his outriders found us. They were almost out of arrows and had not eaten since yesterday morning. They were fairly certain Okehampton was cut off, so they had been on their way to Restormel for more food and arrows when they saw us and came to attack us if that was what needed to be done. Them going to Restormel, of course, was no longer necessary as we immediately shared the bread and strips of burnt mutton we were carrying.

I quickly sent one of my men to carry bread and cheese to his two wounded outriders and to lead their horse cart to the sheep and wains we had tucked away in the hills. He was told to stay with them and tend to them. I made sure he had a fire flint and some of the flower paste from my saddle pouch that makes a wounded man sleepy and soothes the pain of his wound. Two of Michael's outriders rode back with him to help get the wounded men to where we had concealed the sheep and wains.

Michael's two outriders were told to help get their wounded friends settled and dosed with flower paste, cook a goodly supply of bread and burnt meat for both themselves and the wounded men, and then move back to where they could watch the road. They were to warn us if they saw any additional men or supplies coming out of Exeter.

Chapter Fourteen

The noose tightens.

Within minutes of Michael and his men joining us, we had dispatched food and assistance to his two wounded men, fed Michael and his able-bodied men with some of the bread and burnt sheep meat we were carrying, and were once again on our way riding towards the barons' army. Almost immediately one of our outriders galloped in from the north to report that an hour or so earlier he had seen a large force of foragers turn off onto a cart path leading towards one of Devon's large coastal villages to the east of us.

There were, the breathless outrider reported, three empty wains accompanied by a hundred or more walking men carrying swords and shields with only a handful of mounted men riding in front of them as outriders—an altogether very different and much stronger force of foragers than those we had previously encountered.

"Well now, what should I make of that?" I mused out loud as our outrider turned away and rode off to re-join his file. I had said it to myself and did not expect an answer. But I got one from my apprentice sergeant.

"Perhaps they have come to know the size of our fighting groups and have adjusted their foraging parties to fit them?" my apprentice sergeant offered.

I was surprised to hear him speak up. Richard rarely did more than listen and jump with an "aye Lieutenant" when I told him to do something.

"Then why did they send armed men to their own village yesterday and not very many of them?" I asked rather disdainfully to put him in his place.

But he was not cowed.

"Could it be that the men the barons sent foraging always carry weapons and they were sent out before the barons realized the size, or even the existence, of the forces you were sending out to stop them—and now they do?"

Hmm. Richard's a smart lad. Maybe being able to scribe and gobble church-talk does not hurt a man's head as much as everyone thinks.

******

It did not take long to organize my men to go after the big foraging party. I would take Michael and John and their men and harass them from the south; everyone else would harass them from the north.

"Stay with them as long as its daylight," I told the sergeants going north. "And be sure to have your men to pick up all the spent arrows they can find; I will be doing the same to the south."

We ambled and cantered down the cart path with the outrider who had seen the foragers leading the way until we finally caught up with the foraging party. It was bigger company of men than I would have expected, and it was just entering a distant village when we first saw them.

"Best to enter the village carefully and not let them jump out and surprise your men," I announced loudly to the sergeants so that their men could hear as well.

"Keep your distance and do not push your arrows at them unless you can mark your man. We will meet back here after it gets too dark to fight."

It did not work out the way I expected.

We surrounded the foragers in the village, but nothing happened. The mounted foragers moved their horses into a barn and they all formed up around the nearby village well in a turtle with their shields held up and overlapping to prevent our arrows from reaching them. Our knights had done the same thing to protect themselves from the arrows of the Saracen horsemen when I was a crusader.

We, of course, rode closer to put more accuracy on our arrows. The foragers let us ride up quite close before they sprung their surprise—some of them had crossbows. All of a sudden, someone in their turtle gave a shout and a number of crossbows loosed their quarrels all at the same time. Four of our men and two of our horses were immediately hit.

In the blink of an eye three of my men were on the ground within easy shooting distance of the crossbow men sheltering under the turtle's shields and so was a screaming horse. The horse took about ten steps before it went down and took its rider with it, one of John's men. It was chaos with great cheers coming from the enemy turtle and shouts of alarm and confusion from our men.

Things quickly went from bad to worse. Our men galloped their horses forward to aid their fallen fellow archers as was expected of them and they had been learnt to do. Some of them jumped off their horses and began dragging their friends to safety.

Others rushed to those who had fallen and tried to pull them up behind them on their horses so they could ride away with them. John was one of those.

He galloped up to the archer whose screaming horse had fallen and was leaning over to pull him up to sit behind him, when he himself was struck in the side by a quarrel, and fell over on top of the man he was trying to rescue.

What saved many of our men was that it takes so long to reload a crossbow. By the time we got out everyone out of crossbow range we had lost three men killed, including John, and seven men wounded including one who would almost certainly need a mercy. We also lost four horses so that several men will have to ride double the way the Templars sometimes do.

******

After the battle, we withdrew some distance from the village and spent an anxious night camping in the dark and tending to our wounded. We were worried about a counterattack with the foragers creeping up and falling on us while we slept. There was no doubt about it, we would have been quite vulnerable had the men of our enemy's foraging party known where to find us in the dark. As you might imagine, we lit no fires to attract them and the men took turns staying awake and on guard all night long.

In the morning we watched from afar as the foragers left the village and began marching back towards the Exeter road on the cart path. We never did see their riders. They must have slipped out of the village in the night with their horses.

Because we were burdened with our wounded men and had no way to carry them to safety, we were all more than a little relieved to see the enemy foragers begin walking towards the road instead of towards us.

At the very least, had they known where to find us and come for us, they would have almost certainly been able to catch and kill those of our wounded men who were too badly wounded to ride or run—and likely many more or all of us because the company contract, on which every one of us had made his mark, required each of us to burn in hell forever if we ever abandoned a fellow archer while he was still alive.

There was nothing we could do when the foragers began marching away except temporarily leave our four seriously wounded men behind and begin harrying the foragers once again. We did not in any way abandon our wounded, however; as soon as dawn broke, Richard gobbled a prayer at them in church-talk and I sent a galloper named Alex, a fisher man from one of the islands off the coast, to retrieve the outriders' horse cart and the two wounded men in it.

Alex Fisher was told to use the cart to carry all of our wounded men to the safety of the temporary camp where we had our captured wains and sheep herd. We also left the wounded men some of the flower paste that kills pain, some bread and burnt sheep strips to eat, and a couple of bowls for the less-wounded among them, those that did not have crossbow quarrels stuck in them, to use to get water from the little stream that runs near our temporary camp.

Everyone seemed pleased that our wounded men would be so well taken care of, and we all promised to return to make sure they had been rescued. The only thing we did not have was a barber to bleed them.

******

Our wounded men were left where they could not be seen from the cart path, and we caught up with the foragers rather quickly—and began riding with silent menace along both sides of the foragers' closely packed marching column. They had horses pulling the three wains filled with sacks of corn they had taken from the village, and they walked close together so they could raise their shields to form turtle shells to protect themselves from our arrows.

We, of course, rode far enough away so we would not be hit by the crossbow men among them. It was a sight I had never seen before, not even in the Holy Land—a turtle shell of thirty or forty shields walking in front of each wain.

The turtle shells worked for the barons' men until I offered five copper coins to anyone who pushed an arrow into one of the horses pulling the wains. My men, particularly the young ones, responded with enthusiasm to my offer. They began galloping along the column of marching foragers and pushing their arrows at the three wain horses as they rode past them. Pushing arrows while riding was something they knew how to do; one of the wain horses was hit almost immediately.

The foragers stopped marching when our men began riding past, raised their shields to form a turtle, and their crossbow men responded with their bolts. It took a while to get the other two wain horses because the foragers responded by trying to shield them as well. But one after another they were hit to the sound of great cheers from our men.

It was not without cost; one of our archers galloping past the column took a quarrel that went right through his leg and struck his horse, which promptly began screaming and threw him off. Two others of our horses were hit as well and the man who took the quarrel in his leg fell so hard that he broke his arm most painful.

Killing the wain horses did not cause the foragers' to abandon the wains as I had hoped. To my surprise, the wains suddenly began moving down the cart path once again with the foragers themselves pulling them and their wounded sheltering in the wains behind the sacks of corn. The three shield turtles, each in front of a wain its shield carriers were pulling, moved off down the cart path leaving behind the hooves and heads of their quickly butchered wain horses.

For several hours my men and I contented ourselves with riding just out of crossbow range on either side of the cart path the foragers were travelling. The foragers' crossbows made it too dangerous for my horse archers to continue riding in to launch their arrows, particularly since the chance of successfully hitting one of the foragers was low because they would quickly raise their shields to remake their turtle.

The foragers easy passage ended when the cart path went through a wooded area just before it reached the Exeter road. It was Richard's idea.

****** *Apprentice Sergeant Richard*

My horse was stuck in the side by a crossbow quarrel while I was dismounting to try to save one of our men who hit his head and went to sleep when he fell off his wounded horse. It happened when the man was trying to earn a coin by pushing an arrow into one of the wain horses.

I was one of the archers riding behind him and saw him fall. So I pulled up my horse and jumped down to help him as I had been learnt to do. I grabbed the poor fellow under his arms and began pulling him away from the foragers. While I was pulling on him, my horse was wounded and a quarrel hit the sleeping archer in the back of his leg up near his arse.

It all happened very fast and I was not at all afraid until I got him behind a tree so the crossbow men in the foragers' turtle could not see to shoot at us. Then I began shaking like I did at school when it was cold and I was trying to sleep without enough sleeping skins. I did not recognize or even know the name of the archer who almost got me killed. He must have been one of the riders who joined up with us yesterday.

******

After the foragers moved on, I was given a wounded man's horse as a replacement. It was a gelded black and the stirrups hanging from its saddle were too short and could not be adjusted. I was happy to have enough stripes to get it because we had lost so many horses that some of the men with only one stripe were riding double.

All the foragers' wain horses had been hit and everything had quieted down by the time one of the archers brought my new horse to me and handed me the reins. He said it had belonged to his best mate—and he would seen me save Charlie and was glad I would be riding him. The horse's name, he said, was "Brownie." *Charlie? Of course, that must be the name of the archer who went to sleep when his horse went down and almost got me killed.*

"How is Charlie?" I asked as he handed me the reins and I swung myself aboard my new horse.

"Oh he is fine now that you saved him. He is awake and staggering around like he is had too much ale."

I looked at the foragers and their wains in the distance as I climbed into Brownie's saddle and listened to the good news about Charlie. Sitting on Brownie, I could see a great stand of trees before the cart path the foragers were travelling reached the Exeter road. I kept looking at the trees and thinking about them as I rode my new horse to catch up with Lieutenant Raymond so I could resume fetching and scribing for him.

******

"You did good, Richard, real good. The men were cheering you and you deserved it."

"Thank you, Lieutenant. Thank you" ... "uh, Lieutenant, would you consider allowing me to take a few of the men out ahead of the foragers and wait for them where the cart path goes through that stand of trees there in the distance?"

I asked my question most respectfully as I pointed towards the distant trees.

Lieutenant Raymond was a tough looking old greybeard, one of the original archers I had been told. He had rarely before even acknowledged that I existed. This time he eyed me intently and listened as I explained what I had in mind.

Five minutes later we I was galloping off at the head of the nine surviving outriders who had recently joined us. They were quite angry with the foragers for the loss of their fallen sergeant and wounded friends.

They listened and nodded with grim satisfaction when I explained what I had in mind.

Chapter Fifteen

Fighting in the forest.

We did not ride straight up the village cart path to the forest through which the cart path passed. To the contrary, I led my newly assigned men to the left of the stand of trees and we rode all the way around them until we reached the cart path again—and began riding down the path towards the on-coming foragers. We could not see them yet, but we were now galloping hard because we knew they would soon reach us.

"Here. This will do for us."

That was what I shouted to the outriders' chosen man riding by my side as I reined in Brownie. My horse was not the only one tired from our hard ride. I was so stiff and tired that I staggered for a second as I leaped down from Brownie and handed his reins to the outriders' chosen man. *His name was Joe. I do not remember the rest of his name except that his accent suggested he was from somewhere in the midlands. As things turned out, he would never see home again.*

The rest of the outriders were right behind us. They galloped up and began dismounting all around me. There were ten of us in all. Joe and another man stayed mounted and handed around most of their quivers for us to use or hold until they returned. They would lead our horses back up the cart path, tie them up where they could not be seen, and then try to ride back double on one horse in time to re-join us. If they did not return in time, it would be the eight of us against the foragers and their turtles; if they did get back in time, we would be ten.

******

Our horse holders had not returned by the time we could see and hear the approaching foragers. They came around a bend in the cart path and there they were—walking and talking and still pulling the three wains loaded with sacks of corn and their wounded. They did not see us at first because we were hiding behind trees on the south side of the cart path where it narrowed as it passed through the thickest of the forest. Each of us was behind a tree to give us some shelter in case their crossbow men still had quarrels left to shoot.

I picked out a man carrying a crossbow and waited to give my men a chance to mark their targets. *And while I waited I realized I had made a great mistake—I should have told my outriders to push their arrows at men carrying crossbows whenever possible.*

"No sense waiting, lads; get the crossbow men," I shouted and began cheering as I stepped out from behind the tree and pushed an arrow deep into the chest of a crossbow man. He was less than twenty paces away and I clearly saw the bloody arrow tip come out of his back as it knocked him sideways and he went down screaming and flailing about. I would swear he saw me and opened his eyes in disbelief as I pushed my arrow into him.

There were loud cheers and shouts all around me as the eight of us poured arrows into the cluster of surprised men in the road as fast as we could push them out. For a brief moment, some of them attempted to raise their shields to form a turtle. They were too late; they either went down or disappeared into the trees in front of us almost like magic.

When they were gone, we ran through the trees along the cart path to find new victims at the other wains further down the path. This time the foragers did not even try to protect themselves by putting up a turtle shell of shields. They just screamed and shouted, and then ran, as we pushed out arrows and shot them down left and right. It did not take long before the whole column dissolved and it was once again every man for himself.

Eight good archers shooting at close range can push arrows into a lot of people in a very short period of time, and we did. Two or three minutes later there were only dead and wounded men on the cart path and three abandoned wains with the wounded men in them desperately trying to climb out in order to follow their friends who were attempting to escape.

Many of the foragers, particularly the wounded, ran into the nearby trees on the other side of the road; others ran up the road—to find Lieutenant Raymond waiting for them with the rest of our men.

The barons' foragers left seven dead men on the road and five who were too wounded to flee into the trees. I am sure we wounded many more who managed to hide themselves because the trees were so close to the road and the forest so thick.

My men and I were too busy to chase the barons' foragers very far when they scattered and ran. A couple of my men started to plunge into the dense stand of trees after the fleeing foragers, but I called out to them and ordered them to return to the cart path to help unload the barons' wounded men who were still in the wains. We unloaded them and left the barons' dead and wounded men on the cart path for their friends to find.

While we were doing that, Lieutenant Raymond and his men finished off the foragers who had run up the cart path to escape and then rode down it to see what had happened when we ambushed the wains. He was very pleased with what we had done and immediately ordered some of his men dismount so their horses could be used to pull the wains back to what everyone is now calling "our sheep camp," the one in the trees on the west side of the Exeter road where we had stashed our wains and wounded men and flock of sheep.

One thing is certain, praise God—we will not be going hungry for a long time because of all the food in the wains and the sheep we have captured.

It is been hard for me to miss a meal ever since I began attending Bishop Thomas's school and stopped being hungry because I was getting two big meals with meat and an egg and cheese every day, plus extra bread and cheese to carry with me and eat whenever I was hungry. My mum would have been astonished.

Joe was our only casualty. He was killed by a crossbow bolt. We did not even know he had been killed until the other horse holder, a one stripe archer by the name of Luke, galloped up to us with all but two of our horses and reported that he and Joe been attacked from behind by men coming through the forest. Joe, he said, had shouted "I am killed; ride" as he handed him the reins of all but two of the horses he was holding. We found Joe but we never did find the two missing horses.

Chapter Sixteen

A narrow escape.

Lieutenant Raymond's camp had grown from a few dozen men to almost half a hundred in the past three or four days as the circle tightened and our battle groups began coming in contact with one another. I was no longer there as Lieutenant Raymond's apprentice sergeant, his scribe and fetcher. To my great surprise and pleasure, I was now there because I was made the sergeant of what remained of the outriders who had initially been sent to watch the Exeter road and rode with me to the forest ambush, all eight of them.

I was so full of myself from being given my own command that it was all I could do to keep from abusing my newfound powers by giving meaningless orders.

******

Lieutenant Raymond had us tighten the circle around the barons' army even more once there were no villages for the barons to pillage between us and Okehampton. He split the companies of horse archers and outriders who came into his camp into small battle groups consisting of a file or so of men under a company sergeant or file sergeant—and constantly sent us out to harass the baron's army and prevent its foragers from collecting food.

Our orders were to stay in close contact with the enemy and pick off its stragglers, foragers, and couriers. As a result, the barons' men stayed more and more in their camp and we increasingly tightened our encirclement.

It had reached the point where more and more of the barons' foraging parties only pretended to go out searching for food. Indeed, in the past several days archers from some of our battle groups had been riding or crawling right up to the edge of the barons' camp to pick off the sentries and harry the heavily guarded parties of men being sent out to cut grass for their horses. Our noose was tightening.

One result of tightening the circle was that our horse companies began increasingly making contact with each other and camping together under Lieutenant Raymond's direct control. Another was that we became vulnerable to knights trying to make their reputations by leading their men out to ambush us as we crept in to do them harm. It was a dangerous game of cat and mouse and it was not always clear who was the cat and who was the mouse.

******

My outriders and I continued riding and camping with the Lieutenant and the men of his Number One Company after the battle against the turtles. Several mornings later we all rode out together looking for the barons' men until we found some and chased them back to their camp with great shouts and the pushing out of our arrows to kill and wound them. We got so close to the barons' camp that we could see Okehampton Castle in the distance.

It was an important sighting; it meant there were no more villages between us and the castle. We had driven in their foragers and, according to Lieutenant Raymond, now had the barons' army trapped with no sources of additional food.

During the afternoon we linked up with another company of horse archers and joined them in their camp. They had been in their camp for several days and regaled us with stories of how they had been attacking the barons' camp and, in particular, how they had been attacking the parties of men going out to cut grass for their horses. The lieutenant was very pleased.

I thought the lieutenant and the older sergeants would look more favourably on me if my men and I did something similar, so the next morning I gathered up my men and off we went. We were not the only ones—almost every battle group sent its men out in some kind of a raiding party at one time or another every day. Lieutenant Raymond allowed each sergeant to lead his men out to hit the barons' camp on his own. It was expected of us.

Had I been asked, which I was not, I might have suggested it might be better if we all went together and launched our attacks at the same time. On the other hand, I have to admit that I probably would not have mentioned it; I am the most junior sergeant of all. What do I know?

******

We rode out early and I began leading my men towards the barons' camp. Other sergeants and their men were doing the same thing and we all waved and smiled at each other and everyone wished everyone else good hunting. It was very exciting and our camp was full of hustle and bustle. The lieutenant was, as usual, leading one of the attacking groups, a file of men from Number One Company. He smiled and agreed when I asked permission to lead my outriders in a separate foot attack right up to the edge of the barons' camp.

I did not, of course, just lead my men blindly towards the barons' camp until we found some of their men to kill. First, I gathered my men around me and we planned our raid. It was quite helpful that they were all outriders and knew the lands around Okehampton like the palms of their hands. After I made a quick inspection to be sure everyone had their quivers full and at least one extra bowstring under their cap, we all took one last piss. Then we mounted up and I led them off to put a sting on the barons' army.

Each of the little battle groups such as mine was supposed to attack a part of the barons' camp roughly corresponding to our assigned part of the encirclement, and its sergeant was supposed to lead his men to the enemy camp and then lead the attack against it. When we got there, we had do our best to push our arrows into as many enemy men and horses as possible, and then we would mount up and ride away before the barons' men could launch a counterattack.

Attacking the barons' army in this way was the Lieutenant's preferred way of waging war. He said it would bleed them to death from a thousand little cuts. It sounded good to me. It was very exciting.

I led my men north for about an hour and then turned towards the barons' camp. I knew where it was even if I could not see it because I could see

Okehampton Castle in the distance and knew the enemy army was camped on both sides of the cart path leading up to the castle.

Ours would be one of nine or ten such mini-raids this morning on the south side of the barons' camp. According to Lieutenant Raymond, the horse archers assigned to the north side of the enemy army would also be attacking, at least that was what they were supposed to be doing.

My men and I rode easy so the horses would be fresh and strong if we had to run for it. I brought my men, all eight of us, in over the open fields south of Okehampton. I had thought about leading them straight up the cart path, but decided not to do so because more of the barons' men might be positioned there to fight back. Better, I thought, to attack them where they were less likely to be waiting for us in force.

******

My little band of men and I ambled along on our horses for about an hour until we could once again see Okehampton in the distance. Then we stopped at a little stream, so narrow a man could jump over it, and watered the horses and drank our fill. I noticed the men were eating the pieces of bread and burnt sheep strips we had each stuffed into our pouches, so I got mine out and ate with them. We let the horses rest for a while. Then we all pissed and a couple of my men took advantage of the little stream to shite and wash their arses with their hands so they would not get their tunic gowns all sticky and smelly.

"All right, lads, mount up. It is time to push some arrows."

I shouted out the order with a bit of excitement as I mounted my horse and bent over to push the tip of my bow against the ground to bend it and string it. *And why am I so excited and pleased to be doing this?*

It took almost an hour before we made contact with our enemy. I was leading the way and saw the barons' camp as I came out of a little stand of trees. Immediately in front of me were a number of men gathering grass in a large meadow and loading it onto a two-wheeled horse cart. Behind them I could see the tents and wains and horses of the barons' army stretching out into the distance—and all around them were a large number of walking and sitting men.

The grass cutters saw us almost immediately and began shouting and running back to their camp.

"Get them, Lads. Get them," I shouted as I kicked my horse in the ribs and simultaneously drew an arrow out of one of my quivers. In my excitement I selected an armour-piercing "heavy" instead of a "long." It really did not matter; we galloped forward, dropping our reins as we did, and began pushing out arrows as fast as we could.

One after another the grass-cutters closest to us went down as we reached them and pushed arrows into them from up close. At the same time, the barons' camp turned into an absolute beehive of activity. Some men seized weapons and began running towards us; others were running in the opposite direction. A number of them were running for their horses, either to mount them to ride out and challenge us, or to lead or ride them away to the relative safety of the centre of the barons' camp.

I grabbed up my reins before I reached the edge of camp and turned my horse to the right. And not a moment too soon; a few more seconds and I would have been inside the enemy camp and vulnerable. My men were strung out behind me as my horse galloped hard along the outer edge of the camp and I pushed arrow after arrow at the nearest men. I think I hit several before I grabbed the reins instead of another arrow and turned my horse around to make another run along the edge of the camp.

The outriders behind me were still coming as I turned and started back. That was when everything fell apart. I saw it clearly. My last outrider, the tail of my hard-riding little band, was still galloping along the edge of the barons' camp pushing out arrows when his horse suddenly went down as if its legs had been jerked out from under him. He went head over heels tumbling along the ground. I was moving fast and I went right past him at a full gallop and so did the outrider immediately behind me.

Retrieving a fallen rider and carrying him to safety riding double as the Templar knights sometimes do on their big horses, is something we had practiced over and over again. The fallen rider jumps up behind his rescuer and they ride away together. It happens quickly. But somehow retrieving a fallen rider when a man actually goes down turned out to be much harder than doing it in a practice rescue. The confusion and difficulty was ten times greater.

I dropped the arrow I was starting to nock as soon as I saw him hit the ground, jerked my horse around, and started back towards the fallen man. And so did everyone else. It all happened quickly, very quickly. Several of my men had already dismounted and were trying to get the fallen man on his feet by the time I arrived a few seconds later. There was so much confusion that at first I could not tell who had been hurt and who had dismounted to rescue him.

There was no way the archer who had gone down was going to be pulled up on to a rescuer's horse and sit behind him while they both galloped away. The men coming to help him could see he was injured and did not even try. Instead he was picked up and tossed over the neck of his rescuer's horse's on his belly so that his legs hung over one side of his rescuer's horse and his head and arms the other. It was all his rescuer could do to keep the poor fellow from sliding off as they rode away.

While all that was happening, the horse of one of the men who had dismounted to help the fallen rider ran away. That man, at least, was able-bodied and capable of being pulled up behind someone so they could ride away one behind the other like Templars before the men pouring out of the barons' camp could reach us.

Those of us who could pushed arrows out behind us as we rode away and then, without anyone giving an order, we paused when we were far enough away from the camp to compose ourselves. Our fallen man, a one-stripe outrider named Adam, was in bad shape with a broken arm and pains inside his chest. He screamed when he slid off Kenneth's horse and then again as he was being boosted up by numerous helping hands to sit behind him. I saw him grimace in pain with sweat pouring off his face as he rode off holding on to Kenneth for dear life.

Our raid was not a total success; in addition to Adam, one of our horses had been killed and its uninjured rider had to ride double to get back. We were lauded, however, by the men in the camp when we returned with Adam; we had suffered a loss but had inflicted a number of dead and wounded men on the barons' army. Lieutenant Raymond was very pleased.

That evening I listened to the other sergeants as they talked around the campfires and was pleased to be included in the conversation. We all agreed that very few crossbow quarrels had been shot at us; either the barons have very few crossbow men left or they are running out of quarrels. One thing's certain we assured each other with great determination—they would not be receiving any more supplies of quarrels, or anything else, not if we have anything to say about it and maintain our blockade of the enemy camp.

Chapter Seventeen

Disaster strikes.

The next day, greatly encouraged by what happened the previous day and the Lieutenant's response, I led my men out again as did the other sergeants. As usual, we each led our men to the barons' camp separately. This time there would only be six of us going to the barons' camp including me. Adam was wounded and Jacob would be left behind to hold the horses because he was coughing so much that we were afraid the barons' men would hear him and know we were coming.

My men and I got caught in a trap and it was my fault. It happened because I decided to dismount my men, lead them to creep forward to the edge of the barons' camp, and then push arrows at the men and horses in it. One of the sergeants who had brought his men into our camp yesterday said he had already been doing it with his men for several days and it worked very well.

I had heard him talking to the Lieutenant about it. His men, the sergeant claimed, were killing more of the enemy by dismounting so they could push their arrows out further and with more accuracy than was possible while sitting on a horse. The important thing, he said, was to have your men keep your horses close at hand so they could quickly remount them and escape. It sounded like a good idea so I decided to try it.

The next morning we rode from our camp for several hours until we came to a particularly dense forest to the east of the barons' camp. There we dismounted and hobbled our horses in the trees so they would not stray and were not likely to be found unless someone knew exactly where to look for them. I thought we had be able to walk from where we hidden our horses all the way to the barons' camp without being seen.

It had rained the night before and it took us what seemed like many hours to walk through the very wet and thick trees and undergrowth of the forest until we reached the barons' camp. We were moving single file through the trees, and we were wet and cold when we first saw the barons' tents and temporary shelters through the trees.

Everything started to go wrong almost immediately. Twenty paces or so from where we came out of the trees, a skinny young man wearing a ragged tunic was carrying an armful of grass to a couple of horses hobbled near one of the camp's many tents and temporary shelters made of tree branches. Our movement as we began restringing our bows caught his eye and, not being a fool, he started shouting as he ran away towards safety in the middle of the barons' camp.

Pushing an arrow into him so he could not sound the alarm should have been easy. But it was not. Our bowstrings had gotten wet and useless during our walk through the wet and muddy woods. We took our replacement strings out from under our caps and quickly restrung our bows; he was long gone by the time the fastest of my men could push an arrow at him. The alarm had been raised before we had killed so much as a single man or horse.

Sure enough, some of the barons' men on horseback almost instantly galloped up and gathered at the edge of the barons' camp. From the looks of them and the speed with which they arrived, it was probably some kind of a fast-response force the barons had put together to fight off attackers such as we—and some of them had crossbows.

We began pushing arrows at everyone we could see and they had an effect. There was chaos in the barons' camp with horses and men going down left and right. But that did not stop the enemy counterattack.

The horses and riders quickly came charging out of the camp to engage us.

It seemed like time was standing still and that it took the barons' men a lot of time to get organized and charge towards us. In reality, they quickly formed up and charged us. Even so, we had each gone through the best part of a quiver, almost twenty arrows, by the time we ran back into the dense forest from which we had emerged.

Almost immediately our bowstrings once again became too wet to use. We stayed together and ran, slipping and sliding through the damp and muddy forest. Being on foot enabled us to move faster than the horsemen who tried to follow us. It was a tired and muddy, and very elated, band of outriders who slipped the hobbles off their horses and mounted them. Our spirits were high; we had once again wreaked havoc and damage on the enemy and escaped.

We cantered out of the trees into the sunlight to a sight that chilled my heart and caused the hair on my arms to prickle and stand on end—a large number of mounted knights and their squires and men at arms were waiting for us, and not a one of us had a usable string on our bows.

They instantly charged. *My God. Where did they come from?*

* * * * * *

"Quick. Back into the trees. Dismount and lead your horses," I shouted as I wheeled my horse around, dismounted, and strung my bow almost all in one motion. *I, thank God, had carried a second spare bowstring.*

Once again everything seemed to happening very slowly. I selected a "heavy" and pushed it at the thruster in the front of the horde of shouting and sword waving horsemen coming at us. It went low and missed him, but it took his horse in the chest and after a few steps it went down and sent him tumbling towards me. My next arrow took the man who had been riding next to him.

That was was all I could push at them before they reached me. I nocked another heavy as I abandoned my horse and darted off to my left to get deeper into the trees and the heavy brush and tangles that surrounded them—and began shouting to get the horsemen's attention and pushed an arrow at them.

My next arrow missed but it, and the shout I gave as I pushed it out, worked in that it attracted them. Some of them crashed into the forest to pursue me.

They did not get very far because the trees and brush of the forest were so thick, but neither did I because I tried to keep my bowstring from getting wet as I ran. I soon lost all sense of where I was located.

One of my pursuers got close to me almost immediately and there were others behind him. He had the visor up on his helmet so he could see, and was threading his horse through the trees towards me with his sword in his hand. Several other riders were immediately behind him. I could clearly see his red beard and yellow teeth because his mouth popped open when I pushed one of my heavies into his chest with a grunt and another shout.

My pursuer was bending down in the saddle to avoid a tree limb when my arrow hit him. He instinctively raised himself up and the tree limb swept him off his horse. The men right behind him were all shouting and screaming and crashing through the trees as I desperately scrambled away through the heavy forest as if the devil and his disciples were on my heels. And they were—I could hear them crashing through the forest behind me and shouting to each other.

I lost all sense of direction and slipped and fell repeatedly as I vaulted over fallen trees and stepped into deep patches of mud that tried to suck me down. I lost one of my sandals almost immediately and quickly dropped my bow so I could use both hands to push away the branches that grabbed at me and to help me get up when I fell. I had stopped thinking about leading them away from my men. Now all I could think about was getting away from the pain and death coming close behind me. Actually, I did not think at all; I just ran.

It may have been minutes before I stopped crashing through the thick forest and it may have been hours, I really do not know. My hands and feet were cut and bloody by the time I could not go another step and fell trembling to the ground. I was totally exhausted.

Perhaps I fell asleep. I have no idea. The next thing I knew is that I jerked awake when I suddenly heard myself give a loud snore that caused me to raise my head.

For a very brief instant I was confused and did not know where I was. That passed in an instant, and I raised my head and listened—there was nothing around me except the swarm of bitey bugs that formed a cloud over my face and arms. I was covered in mud, my tunic gown was ripped and torn beyond repair, and I had lost my horse and bow and the leather belt with the pouch attached to it that held my coins and food—but I was alive. *Thank you, dear Jesus and all the saints in heaven.*

I put my face down in the mud and rested for an instant, and then slowly and cautiously raised my head up again into the swarm of bugs to look all around me and listen to the forest. Nothing. I closed my eyes to keep the bugs out and slowly put my head back. I did not move quickly, and rightly so; I had been learnt over and over again in Bishop Thomas's school that it is movement that attracts the eye and draws the attention that gets a soldier killed.

Finally, I could not stand the bugs any longer and decided to take a chance by opening my eyes again and slowly and silently sitting up. Still nothing; so I cautiously got to my feet. Suddenly I began itching everywhere and realized I had been cut and scratched and bitten all over my body. I wanted to move away from where I was sitting, but did I dare?

******

I finally decided to move. But which way should I go and how much time did I have before the sun went down? I had no idea. What I did know is that I had to move silently, and that meant slowly and carefully. To my surprise, I discovered I was still wearing one of my sandals. My sandal and my muddy and ragged tunic gown were all I had to my name. I suddenly realized I was desperately hungry and thirsty.

Slowly and carefully, and stopping frequently to listen, I worked my way through the dense forest without any idea of where I was going. For all I knew, I was going in circles. I heard not a sound except the buzzing of bugs, not even the chirp of a bird. Then there was the sharp crack of a tree branch breaking almost next to me.

I turned my head and found myself staring straight into the eyes of a deer not ten feet away. It was a female, at least I thought it was because it did not have horns. I was astonished that I had not seen it. A few seconds later it suddenly turned and began crashing through the forest undergrowth with great leaping bounds—and was joined by four others I also had not seen. *I have got to be more careful.*

Once again I began moving. And just before the sun went down I found what I was looking for—an open area where I could look for the sun and find out which way I would have to walk in the morning in order to go towards the east, away from the barons' camp.

******

All night long I shivered and shook while either sitting with my back to a tree in the darkness or standing up to jiggle my arms and legs in a futile effort to get warm. I thought the night would never end, particularly when it started raining.

It stopped raining by the time morning arrived, and I began to be able to see more and more of the little glade in the forest. To my surprise, there were a number of deer moving about in it. All does without horns. I had never even heard them arrive. But now, at least, I knew which way I needed to walk; or perhaps limp, my bare foot hurts most fiercely every time I take a step.

No more than twenty steps later I realized there was a little stream running through the glade. I had suffered all night long from a great thirst and there had been water only a few steps away. The deer bounded out of sight as I hurriedly limped along the edge of the glade until I came to where the stream ran back into the trees, and drank my fill and then some. It was a great relief and I promptly decided to follow the stream since it seemed to be heading more or less in the direction I wanted to travel.

I walked all day through the thick woods and saw and heard no one. The only thing of importance, at least to me, was that my stomach suddenly began getting great pains and I repeatedly had to stop and shite, and even then my stomach did not stop hurting. Fortunately I was near the stream and could water my arse. I spent another wet and cold night shivering in the forest.

The next morning I once again began following the little stream as it moved towards the south and east. And once again it was slow going until my sore foot became so numb I barely felt it.

Everything changed about half way through the day. For the first time I reached a large open area of farmland. I dare not try to walk straight across it because there was no way I could run back into the woods in time to escape if an enemy on horseback saw me. There was nothing for me to do but stay close to the trees and walk all the way around the edge of the farmland until I could once again start walking south and east.

I saw them when I was about half way around the field. A file of mounted men came out of the trees heading south and east in the general direction of where I wanted to go.

What should I do?

****** *Archer Alfred the wainwright*

"Look. Over there next to the trees," Ed suddenly shouted as he pulled up his horse next to mine and pointed. "Someone's waving."

"String your bow and go over there for a look, Ralph," the sergeant told our chosen man as he too pulled up his horse and held his hand up to his eyes in an effort to see better.

"Take Alfred and Eddie with you. But do not take any chances by getting too close to the trees. We will wait here and cover you if you have to run for it."

We strung our bows and began ambling our horses towards the frantically waving man. Suddenly he began staggering towards us and calling out.

"I think he is wearing an archer's tunic." Ralph said over the familiar pounding sound of our horses' hooves hitting the ground.

"By God; I think you are right," Eddie called back. "Yes; he is." ... "Do you know him?"

"Eddie, ride back and tell the sergeant we may have found one of our own and he looks to be wounded."

Ralph and I kicked our horses in the ribs and began galloping towards the staggering man as he fell and tried to get up; meanwhile, Eddie had wheeled his horse and galloped back to the rest of the party waving his arm in a great circle over his head to summon them. They had seen Eddie turn back and were already moving towards us even before we reached the man who was still waving one of his arms in the air and struggling to stand.

He was definitely wearing an archer's tunic gown and, even though it was torn and muddy, we could see it had three stripes. The man himself was in no better shape. He was caked with mud from head to toe, wearing only one sandal, and covered with scratches and the big red welts of bug bites.

"Who are you?" I shouted as I dismounted and handed my reins to Ralph so my horse would not bolt.

****** *Richard*

I tried to run out into the field when they got close enough to see that they were, indeed, some of our archers. For some reason I was terribly afraid behind my eyes that they would turn and ride away. But they did not.

"I am Richard, the Lieutenant's apprentice sergeant, his clark," I croaked as I tried to stand up and one of the riders dismounted. I was crying and laughing at the same time. "It is me, Richard; I am Richard."

A man who had dismounted and was trying to help me stand up was surprised and said as much.

"It is Richard, who used to be the Lieutenant's apprentice, Ralph; the young'un who sergeants the outriders."

The man who dismounted said this to the horseman with surprise in his voice. Behind them I could see the rest of the party galloping up. For some reason, I noticed that they all had their bows strung.

"They said you were dead; said you saved them, did not they?" the archer said to me with wonderment and approval in his voice as he held me up and the other archers began returning their arrows to their quivers and dismounting all around us.

Dead? "I am not dead," I insisted as I swayed and would have fallen if someone had not caught me and held me up. My right foot which had been so numb suddenly began to hurt most painful.

"Food? Do you have any food?" I gasped as I tried to stand on one leg and hold my hurting foot off the ground.

******

They found a piece of bread for me from someone's pouch and helped me onto the horse of the dismounted archer. His name, he told me, was Alfred, and he used to be a wainwright's apprentice before he ran away and joined the archers. I vaguely recognized him from camp but did not know him at all.

Alfred mounted behind me to hold me in the saddle. I was able to get my left foot into Alfred's stirrup even though it was too short, but my right foot hurt so much when I tried to put it in the other stirrup that I just let my leg dangle. It was a painful ride to our new camp. Fortunately, it did not take as long as I had expected; we had moved closer to Okehampton and the barons' army since I had led my outriders on our ill-fated raid.

Our arrival was quite pleasing. I did not see him go, but one of the men must have ridden on ahead to tell the Lieutenant they were bringing me in, and that I would need a clean tunic gown, and maybe a bleeding to help me recover if a barber was available.

There was much shouting and men coming to gather around us as we rode into camp. The Lieutenant himself came to greet me and help me climb down off Alfred's horse, and steadied me when I failed to stand on one leg and started to fall to the ground. And, of all people, my old school chum, George, Captain William's son, was there with his outriders beaming their approval. The last I had heard of George, he was off with his outriders to watch the London road. He must have come in while I was away.

My own outriders, the ones I had taken over sergeanting when John fell, all came rushing up with big smiles on their faces. I found myself counting them and coming up short. Several were missing.

"Who did not make it?" I croaked.

Chapter Eighteen

The Barons march.

The air was heavy with anger and disbelief as the barons gathered in the camp they had established where the cart path to Okehampton turns off from the road to Exeter. Many of their foraging parties had not returned and some of those that had returned had come back with dead and wounded men instead of sheep to slaughter and sacks of corn. It was not at all what the barons had been led to believe would happen, and they were not happy about it.

"First our baggage train is heavily damaged, and now the replacement supplies you promised to provide us from your villages are slow in arriving."

The white-bearded lord glared at the Earl of Devon as he said it and pounded his fist on the wooden plank that had been taken from the side of a wain and set up in the tent as a table. His nephew was one of the seriously wounded.

"We have not even gotten to Cornwall and already we are suffering heavy losses. Some of my best men have already been killed and wounded and I lost two more yesterday when they went out to cut grass for our horses. My men know they will soon be running out of bread. They will soon be hungry and start deserting if we do not do something."

"Do not blame me for the attack on your baggage train. I am not responsible for your failing to guard it properly," the red-faced Earl of Devon retorted. He was not used to someone shouting at him.

"Besides, you were able to quickly retake your baggage wains, were not you?" the earl added.

"Yes," came the angry answer, "but only after we lost almost all of our draught horses and much of our corn supplies were scattered on the ground. We had to use some of our riding horses to pull the wains, for God's sake. And then those peasant bastards followed us all the way back here and picked off some of our men with their arrows. You told us Devon was peaceful and Cornwall was weak."

He glared at the Earl and slapped the table as he made his accusations. Devon did not back off.

"Well, I admit I did not expect them to come out of Cornwall. But it just shows how weak they are—they have no knights to fight us so they have to sneak around and ambush us with their arrows. That was why I have begun sending much stronger parties out to my villages including men with crossbows.

"Besides, their being here in Devon instead of waiting for us in Cornwall should make things easier. They cannot be in two places at once, can they? If they are scattered about in small bands around here, we will be able to walk in and take Cornwall without even having to fight a real battle—though I admit they will probably have the relics hidden somewhere, probably at Restormel, that we will have to take with a siege. On the other hand, without knights to stiffen them and lead them, they may just surrender to save themselves." *Not that it will save them.*

The possibility that they would lose never entered the barons' minds; they were angry at being inconvenienced by commoners who did not fight fair.

******

It was not until a few days later that the full impact of the horse archers was finally understood by the barons. They now knew that many of the foraging parties which had not yet returned, would never return.

They themselves were alive and still did not fully realize what their men were facing because it would have been beneath their dignity to go out foraging or cutting grass. And they were, at least so far, well fed and, truth be told, so were their men—because of the supplies that had been salvaged from their baggage train and the corn and sheep some of their foragers had been able to bring in despite the constant attacks by Cornwall's archers.

Almost all of the barons had experienced fighting in France and knew it was likely that Cornwall would be stripped of food by the time their army arrived. That was why they had intended to carry enough food into Cornwall to last the entire fighting season.

The loss of much of their baggage train had been an unpleasant surprise. It resulted in the Earl of Devon quickly offering to make up their losses with the food reserves of his own villagers. Of course he did; he stood to gain more than the others if they got the relics—he would get Cornwall and the lands of Okehampton in addition to the restoration of his baronial powers. Now, however, it increasingly looked as though he would not be able to make up the shortfall in food. It was all the fault of the archers of Cornwall.

But all was not lost for the barons despite the large knight-led parties not being able to bring in enough corn and livestock to support a prolonged campaign. Those of the foragers and grass cutters who did return reported that they had fought fiercely and had inflicted great casualties on the archers even when they were unable to bring in any food. This encouraged the barons.

"We would not need so much corn and mutton, do not you see?" said one of Devon's supporters from amongst the rebel lords.

"Now we can defeat them quickly because we have already hurt them badly in the fights with our foragers and grass cutting parties. Skirmishing with our foragers is one thing, fighting us in real battles is another; those villagers will melt away like butter in the sun when they face a proper army. One charge and the war will be over."

Some of the barons were not so sure; not all of their men had returned claiming to have killed large numbers of the archers who had bloodied them and all too often sent them back empty-handed. In the end, however, they too agreed with the new plan—to march on to Cornwall two days later with the supplies of food they had in hand.

The barons agreed to the new plan because they knew that an army without armoured nobles and knights to raise their banners and lead it into battle could not win a war. Never had; never would. The conquest of Cornwall would be over quickly. Then they would settle into sieges until the relics were surrendered.

Besides, they told each other as they walked away from the meeting, had not their priests assured them that God was on their side and they would surely win because they would be fighting to get the relics God had intended for the Church? That they were really fighting so King John would restore their baronial powers was never mentioned.

******

The army was supposed to begin marching for Cornwall immediately after the men awoke and broke their fast on the second morning after the meeting. It was a reasonable thing for the barons to agree to do because they wanted to get their army into Cornwall and seize the relics before they ran out of food.

It did not happen, the army leaving immediately after the men finished eating their breakfasts two days later. Each of the barons expected the others to march while he finished breaking his fast and striking his tents. As a result, no one marched until the sun was directly overhead. It is the kind of thing that happens when an army has no clearly identified commander to tell it what to do.

We could not see the barons' army as the galloper rode into our camp two afternoons later and shouted the news that the barons were marching towards Cornwall, all we could see in the distance was the castle itself silhouetted against the sky and the white puffy clouds that were gathering to the north. His news quickly flowed through our camp.

"They are on the move; they are on the move."

Almost immediately Lieutenant Raymond called an "all-sergeants" meeting and we began hurriedly breaking camp.

****** Richard

An hour later, George and I were riding together and once again talking about everything from our school days together at Restormel to our similar surprises at being told by Lieutenant Raymond that we were to sergeant one of the company's two groups of outriders, and our experiences when we did. George had brought his outriders into the camp while I was lost in the woods and had spent much of the next two days after my return watching over me like a mother cat watches over her kittens or a bitch over her pups. My foot still hurt, but at least I could now ride and be the sergeant of what was left of my men.

We were riding a mile or so ahead of the main column of horse archers with a couple of our outriders riding with us in case we needed gallopers with fresh horses. The rest of our outriders were in their usual positions—ranging far out in front of the column or miles off to either side of it. Most of them were off to our right where the barons' army was marching on the road to Cornwall

"I wonder if we will see any of our old boys from school?" I asked George as I shifted in my saddle to get more comfortable.

"Oh, it is almost certain we will. The last I heard, four of them are apprentice sergeants with our main force in Cornwall. And, of course, the other two, Alfie and Pudge, are in Cyprus fetching and scribing for Harold and Yoram."

"Uh oh, here comes trouble." It was the Lieutenant and a couple of men riding out from our main column; and they were riding hard to catch up with us. We reined in our horses and waited for them.

Something was up for sure and we both know what probably triggered it. About thirty minutes ago a couple of our outriders had come in and confirmed that the barons' army was still travelling without outriders. George, as the higher ranking sergeant because I had only three stripes and he had four, immediately sent one of our fresh riders galloping to the Lieutenant with the news.

"Hoy lads," Lieutenant Raymond said as he pulled his horse to a stop next to us. "I got your message, George. It sounds encouraging. I want you two to ride out with me to take a look at the barons' army. I want to know how spread out they are and where they have got their baggage train." *Encouraging? Oh God; we are going to fight for sure.*

******

George and I rode with the Lieutenant towards the road to Cornwall on which the barons' army was travelling. A couple of the Lieutenant's men rode with us. They were leading a couple of extra horses as remounts in case any of ours were hit or went lame.

The road to Cornwall on which the barons' army was travelling was actually little more than a cart path once it turned off from the main road between London and Exeter just south of Okehampton. We maintained it where it went through Okehampton's lands. After it entered the Earl of Devon's lands again, however, it became quite rough and remained that way until it reached the Launceston ford and entered Cornwall. Then it became a real road once again.

According to outriders who had come in and brought the news, the barons' entire army, including the much-reduced number of women and merchants who were still with it, was on the march. It was reportedly moving slowly even though the barons had left some of their empty wains behind, more than likely because the army had no supplies for them to carry and no horses to pull them.

Lieutenant Raymond rode between us and we talked the entire time until we went up on to a little hill and, from there, could see the barons' army strung out along the cart path running through the trees. The two men with the extra horses followed behind us. It was actually the most I had ever talked to the Lieutenant. He wanted to know more about our skirmishes and what we had been learnt at Thomas's school.

George did most of the talking, being as he had four stripes and me but three. But I learnt a lot. It was the first I had actually heard George talk about what happened to him during the fight with the French. *And then and there I decided to practice swimming again in the river.*

It was certainly the biggest army I had ever seen. George, however, said it looked quite a bit smaller than when he would first seen it pass on the London road, and it was moving even slower. Little wonder in that, if the stories we had heard at camp were even half true, George and his men had whittled its numbers down quite a bit and killed many of its horses.

George and I talked about what we had seen and how we might use our men as we rode back to camp. The Lieutenant did not join us; he seemed deep in thought and rode ahead of us.

"Uncle Raymond," George called out to him when we were almost back to our camp. "Richard has an idea; two ideas, actually."

******

Less than an hour later every able-bodied man in our camp was mounted. We ambled out of the camp leading every available spare horse so we had have as many replacements as possible.

Our destination was a round and treeless hilltop overlooking the cart path where it goes through a large area of Devon farmland about ten miles before the cart path to Cornwall reaches the Launceston ford. At its current rate of speed, the baron's army would not reach the ford until late tomorrow morning. We brought all the arrows in our camp with us as well as all the knightly banners our men had taken in the course of our skirmishes.

We reached the hilltop before sundown and made a dry camp. There was a stream a couple of miles away flowing towards the Tamar so it was not a problem getting water for the horses and men. The cart path to Cornwall was about three miles to the south and clearly visible. Our camp was on the far side of hill so it could not be seen from the cart path.

Late the next morning we began to see signs that the barons' army was approaching. An advance party of perhaps twenty knights and mounted men came into view first. It was the barons' idea of an early warning force. We saw no outriders.

"Well, that was something new," George observed as we shaded our eyes with our hands and watched while standing next to our horses. "When I first saw them on the London road, they did not even have an advance party."

The barons' advance party was still in sight when the riders at the front of the main column came into view. It was our intention to stand here and watch them until they stopped for the night—because where the barons made their camp for the night would determine where we would position our false army when we rode out to confront them in the morning.

"My numbering and summing has about forty of them for every one of us," said George rather gleefully after the Lieutenant assembled all the sergeants and told us how we were going to fight in the morning. "We have got them by the bollocks for sure."

George meant his encouraging words. I, however, was not nearly so confident in the plan I had suggested, and, from the looks on their faces as they watched the marching army passing in the distance, neither were the archers and many of their sergeants. We knew how we had fight; but how would they fight?

******

Early the next morning we lined up all our men on their horses along the top of a hill so we had be visible to the barons' army in the distance when the sun came up. Knightly banners were fluttering all along our line of horsemen even though they were not ours and we had no knights among us. It may have worked—a party of riders was coming towards us from the barons' camp. *Well, now at least we will know if what we were learnt about knights and nobles in our school applies to the real world.*

"Well lads, here they come," Lieutenant Raymond said. "It is time for us to ride down there and see if Richard is right."

Lieutenant Raymond and George and I kicked our horses in the ribs and rode down the hill towards the four men who were riding towards us. We galloped in an effort to meet them far enough forward of our line of horsemen. It would not do to have our visitors get close enough to see that the knightly and baronial banners our many were displaying were not held by knights and barons and their standard-bearers. We were carrying shields and swords taken from the weapons we had captured; our longbows were nowhere to be seen.

Our meeting was initially quite cordial, although the splendidly attired leader of our visitors and his men could barely contain their surprise at seeing our plain tunic gowns with the stripes of our ranks on their fronts and backs.

"Good day to you; I am Robert of Frodesham, herald of the Earl of Chester who commands the army you see before you."

"And good day to you, Sir Robert. I am Raymond of Okehampton, lieutenant to William, Earl of Cornwall, on whose lands you have placed your army without my lord's permission. Why have you ridden out to meet us?"

"Why to challenge your lord and his army to combat, of course, so that God may judge who is in the right."

Those were the words we had hoped to hear. What Bishop Thomas and Angelo Priestly told us at school about the customs and pride of the nobles and their knights was true; this might work.

Good old Lieutenant Raymond answered as George and I had coached him to answer—with an agreement that would prick their pride.

"The Earl of Cornwall sets much store in the Will of God, Sir Robert. So we agree—on the condition that the battle begins within the next three hours in the open area a couple of miles behind this hill where we will be waiting for you.

"We will wait for you there for three hours. But I must tell you, Sir Robert, that the Earl of Cornwall and his men think your Earls of Chester and Devon and their knights are cowards. And being cowards they will send their villagers and servants forward to fight for them while they cower and piss themselves in the rear because they are too afraid to face even the common men of Cornwall.

"Accordingly, if the fears of your commander and his friends are still holding you back from engaging us by the time the sun is directly overhead, we will turn and ride away in contempt—and send messengers to the king telling him how Lord Chester and his fellow barons and their knights were cowards who avoided combat because they were afraid to fight even a handful of Cornwall's mounted villagers."

Then, as Richard and I had suggested, and he had three times practiced, Lieutenant Raymond leaned forward, poked his finger at Chester's herald, and really rubbed in his insults.

"In other words, my dear Sir Robert, we are here and we are waiting for you— and if you do not come to fight us, the king and everyone else in England will know your Lord Chester and his fellow barons and knights are cowards and unworthy of your lands and titles."

Sir Robert's eyes and those of his companions absolutely sparkled with anger at all Lieutenant Raymond's insults—and he agreed to the terms through clenched teeth. It was the only thing he could do. Any effort to suggest changes to the terms would be seen as trying to avoid fighting us.

"Well, let us hope this works," Lieutenant Raymond said as we cantered back to our men and Sir Robert and his companions rode away with as much arrogance and disdain as they could muster.

Chapter Nineteen

The challenge is accepted.

We cantered back up the hill to our waiting men. A few minutes later we began leading the men to where the Lieutenant wanted them positioned for the beginning of the battle—and he began explaining to each of the sergeants what he and his men were to do when the barons attack and the fighting starts. There was plenty of time so on the way we stopped at the stream for water and something to eat. Four of our outriders remained behind to bring us word of the barons' army.

"Three hours? Well they certainly would not have much time to get ready and march so far, will they?" George commented with a smile as we watched our horses drink—and fed them corn from our caps after we had carefully removed our bowstrings so our horse would not eat them.

"Yes," I said with an answering smile. "They will have to hurry to get to the battle and wear themselves out, would not they?"

******

The initial hillside position Lieutenant Raymond picked for his men, all of them riders on good horses, would form the first battle line for the barons to attack. It looked to be about five miles from the barons' encampment. Reaching it would require the barons' army to either march over recently ploughed land or go around it and add several miles to their march. Either way, they had have to hurry to reach us by the appointed hour.

George and I did not take our men to join the Lieutenant's initial battle line. After we watered our horses, Lieutenant Raymond sent us with all of our available men back to join the four outriders already watching the barons' encampment. We had a new assignment for ourselves and our outriders. George was in command of Raymond's outriders because of his four stripes; I was his lieutenant with three. It was exactly as I suggested.

We did not even get back to the outriders watching the barons' camp when we met one of the outriders we had left to watch it. He was riding hard and barely slowed down to shout his message as he went galloping past us.

"They are coming. They are coming."

His report caused George and I to step up our speed. We and our outriders went from our horses ambling towards our observers waiting on the hill ahead of us to cantering towards them. A second outrider came tearing past us just before we reached the two outriders remaining on the hill.

"All them buggers is heading this way" was all we could hear him shout as he galloped past us without slowing down. It was very exciting.

We saw everything as soon as we came far enough around the side of the hill where our two remaining outriders were waiting—the barons had accepted Raymond's challenge; they were leading their entire army towards where they expected to find Cornwall's army.

What we saw of the barons' army appeared to be quite chaotic. Horsemen and men on foot were hurrying towards the proposed battleground, and some of the men on foot were having trouble keeping up with the banners carried by the horsemen they were following. They did not stop to water their horses at the little stream we had been using, although most of the walking men would undoubtedly scoop up a few handfuls as they went past it.

****** *Raymond*

I sent George and all my outriders back to watch the barons' army. Richard went with him as his deputy. I sent the two lads because they understand the plan right well and are less likely to move too quickly and cause the barons to return to their encampment before they are finished. *Of course they understand it; it was Richard's idea, was not it?*

My men and their horses and weapons are as ready as I can get them. It is a pity I do not have more men here to fight the barons. All I have are about one hundred men who can ride and that includes the lightly wounded men who can sit a horse.

I also have about twenty remounts that are being led in case some of our horses go down. They are all I have and there is nothing I can do about it except fight with what I have got. It is a pity that we did not bring our caltrops and stakes and such to sprinkle around in front of us, but we did not and there is no use crying over spilt ale.

****** *Raymond*

Two hours later, the farmland opening out in front of us was covered with the barons' men and horses, and they were all coming this way, just as we had hoped. There certainly were a lot of them. It looked more like a disorganized nest of ants some farmer had dug up rather than an army, except all the ants were coming towards us and carrying weapons. They ought to be exhausted, the men on foot at least, for how fast and far they have had to come on a hot summer day.

Well, we are ready for them, are not we? My men have walked off the distance and put out little piles of rocks to mark the kill zone if we use our longs while we are mounted. They have also done the same on two of the hillsides behind us where we will make additional stands after they push us off this hill—and in doing so move themselves further and further away from their encampment when we flee and they pursue us. At least that was the plan.

******

It would not be much longer. The knights and other horsemen are obviously getting ready to charge up the hill to reach our line and come to grips with us. They have seen how few we are and appear to have taken our insults to heart—they are forming up to charge us on horseback instead of sending their men on foot in first.

The fools still think they are going to fight a pitched battle the way they fight the French.

My archers and I watched as the various barons and knights rode up and down in front of their little groups of followers. No doubt they were exhorting them with promises and threats and such.

A few minutes later they began walking their horses towards us in preparation for their grand charge. So far, so good—they have not sent their foot or crossbowmen forward, not yet at least. Hopefully that means their crossbow men are out of quarrels and the knights have taken our questioning of their bravery as we had hoped—badly—so they had become foolish and charge at us on their horses with their men running along behind them.

The barons did not seem to have been put off by seeing so few of us. I had been afraid they would think it was an attempt to gull them because I had more men hiding somewhere to fall upon them. I only wish that I did. On the other hand, waiting here for them to charge certainly was an attempt to gull them.

"String your bows." I shouted my order and all the sergeants and chosen men immediately repeated.

I did not order my men to dismount. Of course, I did not. They might get better distance pushing out their arrows when they have both feet on the ground, but they are going to need to pull their horses around and leave in a hurry to ride to our next position.

******

A horn sounded from somewhere in barons' ranks below us and then another; their banners dipped, and the barons' mounted knights began walking their horses forward. Their foot followed behind them in a great disorganized mob. The barons and knights were still walking their horses as they passed our range rocks and moved into our kill zone. A few more feet and they had undoubtedly stop and wait for the signal to begin their grand charge. I had no intention of letting that happen.

I raised my arm high over my head and shouted.

"Nock your arrows and choose your man."

The sergeants and chosen men repeated it loudly as they should. Then I dropped my arm and shouted "push" … "push" … and kept shouting it as we unleashed a stream of arrows on the horde of men assembled below us.

Our arrows fell upon the riders in front of us as if we were wielding God's hand of death. There were always hundred arrows in the air as our men loosed them as fast as they could with great pushes and grunts.

The mass of men below us on the gentle hillside twisted and twitched as our arrows streamed down on to them. The reaction and movement was particularly great among the men nearest the banners in the centre. We could clearly hear the screams and shouts and other loud noises as men were hit and horses bolted. There was instant chaos and confusion.

We each got off at least five or six arrows before the surprised riders below us even began lurching forward. That soon settled into a determined charge with the horses that fell and their unhorsed riders tripping and knocking over those that were not otherwise hit.

I stopped pushing out arrows as they got closer, raised my arm, and tried to imagine how soon the thrusters at the front of our attackers would reach us. Then it was time to go.

"Fall back" ... "Fall back"

My sergeants and chosen men had expected my order and echoed it as we wheeled our horses around and galloped back about towards our next position, a little rise behind us. We turned around as we rode and loosed arrows over our shoulders all the way to our next position. Almost all of us made it, although I did see one of my men get cut down. The fool stayed to shoot an extra couple of arrows and did not turn his horse and run until it was too late. A knight got him with his lance.

That was when things started to go wrong. We reached our rally point with its range stones and turned our excited and blowing horses to once again face our enemy. Most of our pursuers were not even close when we turned to face them once again. Our problem was the few of our sword-waving pursuers who were well-horsed and able to stay close behind us after we turned and retreated to our new position. A couple of them crashed into our disorganised new line and took some of our men with their swords.

Our archers finished them off before they did too much damage. But our newly established line was confused and not ready to put enough arrows into the sword and lance-bearing knights and other horsemen who had followed their thrusters. *Damn, they are too close.*

"Disengage and fall back to the next position; go for their thrusters," I shouted as I put a "heavy" deep into an approaching horse.

As I hauled my horse around to run for it, I watched the horse I had just hit slew around and fall heavily onto its shoulder as its left leg went out from under it and roll over. The eyes of the brown-bearded knight riding it met mine for a brief instant as he went down. He was still holding tightly to his sword and shield when his horse rolled over him.

* * * * * *

I was still catching my breath when I realized that only about seventy of my horse archers had reached our second rally position. I was so surprised I counted again. We must have lost more men than I thought when the knights' thrusters got in among us with their swords.

About the only good thing was that most of the barons' horsemen pulled up after we abandoned our first fall-back position. It suddenly struck me that the knights might have succeeded in pushing us out of our first fall-back position because they had the visors on their helmets down and could not see enough to be worried when we began pushing arrows at them and their horses.

Not all of the barons' horsemen pulled up. A handful of fools among them still did not appreciate the power of our longbows and continued pursuing us even after we abandoned our first fall-back position and galloped here to our second. They had made a bad mistake because we had enough time to prepare to receive them.

When they got close enough they discovered that our iron-tipped "heavies" will indeed penetrate armour. And there were so few of them that each received the attention of multiple archers. It was a forlorn hope for glory and distinction, and the six or seven knights who kept coming all went down.

Most of the barons' horsemen were not so foolish. They turned back and began assembling, perhaps to prepare for another charge, where they thought our arrows could not reach them. Because of the little rise on the side of the hill blocking my view, I could not see the barons' men on foot even though they were most likely coming up behind the milling crowd of heavily armed enemy horsemen in front of us.

"Longs and nock," I shouted and my sergeants once again loudly repeated as was expected of them. And then we all watched and cheered as one of the men who had somehow not fallen back with us, suddenly came bursting through the barons' line and galloped safely towards ours.

I raised my arm and gave the order as soon as he was clear.

"Push." ... "Push." ...

Once again the air was filled with the hum and swishing sound of our arrows and there was again great confusion among those receiving them. This time, however, instead of charging forward, they pulled their horses around and scrambled to fall back. They were too tired to be enthusiastic and their foot was still nowhere in sight. They left behind a number of unhorsed men on the ground and struggling to get on their feet to follow them.

"Begin the wounded bird," I shouted, and my sergeants repeated. Then I raised my arm and pointed it at the barons' men as I kicked my horse in the ribs and it started ambling towards the enemy. But then I pulled my horse to a stop and turned around, as if I was in great dismay, when only a few of my men followed me.

One after another my men peeled off and began galloping away towards the rear. I shook my fist at them in despair and motioned for the few who had followed me to retreat.

What happened next was inevitable. The barons' horsemen gave a great cheer and surged forward to chase after us. They knew a victory when they saw one and were yelping and howling as if they were chasing a running fox; what they did not know was that they were chasing a "wounded bird."

Chapter Twenty

Time to begin.

Sergeant George and all of the available outriders stood on the hill next to their horses and watched as little dabs and trickles of the barons' army, mostly wounded men, began returning to the camp they had so hurriedly left some hours previously. I was the only one not standing; I was sitting on my horse because my foot still hurt. It ached most fiercely even when I was in the saddle, but it pained me even more when I put my weight on it and tried to walk.

We were on the hill with our surviving outriders, all seventeen of us, watching the barons' encampment on the cart path to Cornwall. Our initial task was merely to warn the Lieutenant if anything significant happened at the camp, such as reinforcements coming or going. That was easy. Our subsequent task was not—to attack the encampment whilst its fighting men were gone and wreak as much death and destruction on it as we could on the horses and oxen pulling the barons' supply carts.

George was the senior sergeant. It was my plan but it would be George's decision as to how soon we would attack the barons" encampment. The problem, of course, was that if we acted too soon, the barons' army would rush back to protect the camp before we could do much damage. We were, therefore, supposed to wait up here on the hill until the barons and their men were far enough away so that they could not return in time to save their baggage train. All we knew for sure was that Raymond intended to keep withdrawing his men so long as the barons continued to follow him further and further away from their camp.

At first we primarily saw some walking wounded returning to the camp. And, of course, we periodically did more than watch them. Either George or I would lead some of our outriders down the far side of the hill when we saw someone coming or going on horseback. We went after the riders and tried to shoot them down from a safe distance—out of range of their swords and lances.

A few of the mounted returnees were able to gallop past us; most did not. Others rode off to the east away from both us and the barons' encampment. Somehow, perhaps from the way they carried themselves and direction they were riding and walking, we could tell they were going home. We did not bother the returning walking wounded or those who were leaving.

All of a sudden, we could see a notable increase in the number of walking wounded and returnees in the distance.

"There must have been a fight," George noted as we stopped to catch our breaths after a brief chase. "And we are only seeing the cowards and the walking wounded; there must be a lot of dead and seriously wounded men up there with the Lieutenant."

"And look at that," George said a few minutes later as he pointed at a small group of riders in the distance, some of whom were obviously wounded. "All their tunics are the same colour; one of the barons or knights must have abandoned the fight and left his foot to their fates."

It was the first organized group of returnees we had seen. After a few moments of watching the distant riders, George made up his mind.

"I think it is time for us to start while the baggage train is still unguarded. We will do as you suggested and start at the front and work our way to the rear. I will take the far side; you and your lads take this side."

******

Our horses, all gelded rounceys and natural amblers, ambled down the hill in two lines, with my outriders following me and George's following him. We stayed together as we turned left at the bottom of the hill and rode in a big circle to get around the barons' encampment and reach the cart path on which the barons' army had been travelling.

Every man's bows was strung, a spare bowstring was under every cap, and we were each carrying as many quivers of arrows as we could carry. We each also had a sharp pointed stick which we had use wherever possible on the barons' horses and livestock so we would not waste our arrows. I myself had no less than six full quivers of arrows, and so did most of my men—two on my back and four hung over my horse in front of my saddle and secured to it so they would not slip off.

"Good luck, George," I said with a great deal of emotion as we leaned out of our saddles towards each other and shook hands; "the same to you, old boy," was his equally fervent response.

With that we began leading our two little files of men down the cart path towards the barons' camp; my men and I on the right hand side of the path; George and his men on the left. I had completely forgotten about my sore foot as I nocked an arrow and held my reins between my teeth as my fully rested rouncey ambled towards the camp.

******

We started slowly with a lot of shouting and motioning as George and I had agreed. I pushed an arrow into the side of an ox but I did not shoot at the wide-eyed man and the boy on seat of the cart to which it was hitched. I did not ignore them either.

"Either start running up the road or die here," I shouted as I aimed an arrow at the man and motioned them towards the camp spread out behind them.

They ran. And we followed right on their heels as we swept into the baron's camp. Everyone we came to was given the same shouted order to either run or die, and we either shot down or stabbed our spears into every horse or ox we could reach.

Within a few short seconds there were screaming and shouting men and women everywhere as desperate civilians and wounded men abandoned their tents and campsites, and ran down the cart road in front of us in a desperate effort to escape. We were an unexpected wave of violence that swept into one end of the camp and flowed through it towards the other end.

The going got slower and slower as we reached the heart of the camp, but only because there were more people to send on their way and more horses and oxen to kill. There was some scattered resistance as some of the barons' sick and wounded picked up their weapons and tried to fight back. But mostly there was a great panic and just about everyone ran. The only people we pushed arrows into were those who picked up weapons. There was no organized resistance.

Our bloody destruction of the camp seemed to go on forever. In fact it did not take very long at all. The panic was contagious and people ran in every direction except towards us as we moved inexorably forward from one cart-pulling horse or ox to the next. We could see people streaming out of the camp in all directions, but most of them were running or riding away from us in the direction from whence they had come.

The people in the barons' camp ran back the way they had come because we had deliberately avoided simultaneously attacking the eastern end of the huge encampment. We left it unmolested so they would have someplace safe to go if they decided to run. Bishop Thomas had made much of doing that in our school.

I was almost out of arrows, and I had a slice in my leg and three wounded men by the time we reached the far side of the devastated camp. I was exhausted and panting hard and so was my horse and all of my men. I could see hundreds of people hurrying down the road towards distant London.

"Hoy Richard," George called as he cantered up to me with several of his outriders following him. "Are you fair?"

****** *Lieutenant Raymond's wounded bird*

The barons' horsemen immediately began chasing after us when they saw me turn back to follow my fleeing men. Somehow they never were quite able to catch us just as a fox is never quite able to catch a bird pretending to be wounded leads a fox further and further away from its nest.

There was little wonder that they were not able to catch us. Our horses were generally of a better quality, and certainly more rested. Several times one or two of the barons' thrusters on good horses almost caught us, only to go down when a horse archer turned around in his saddle and pushed an arrow into him or his horse.

We did not sit on our horses and wait when the last of the barons' horsemen finally stopped chasing us and pulled up their exhausted horses to rest them. Not at all.

I gave the order and we turned around began moving back the way we came until the barons' men were in range. They were all riders since they had left their foot far behind. We again showered them with arrows and they moved backward with slightly fewer men and horses. We repeated this two more times. The second time they backed up and we again began moving towards them, is when they finally broke and began streaming away.

Acting like a wounded bird and constantly retreating as if we were wounded and distressed had worked quite well. The barons' army had followed us further and further away from their encampment and strung themselves out into a disorganized mob that we could turn on and begin destroying. And that was exactly what we did.

As soon as the last of the barons' riders stopped chasing us and turned back, I gave the order for my men to turn their horses and give chase. Unlike those of the knights and their riders, our horses were all rounceys bred for speed and stamina and, above all, the ability to amble. Moreover, They were also relatively fresh and well ridden as we turned around and charged after the fleeing knights and began shooting them down as we reached them.

For the barons' army, it quickly became panic with every man for himself with the devil taking the hindmost.

The disorganized and fleeing knights rode right through their exhausted foot soldiers and kept on going. They were desperate to escape and could not—we were galloping up behind each fleeing rider and putting an arrow into him or his horse, and then moving on to the next fleeing knight and repeating the process. We totally ignored the barons' foot.

Most of the barons' foot soldiers, village levies almost all of them, had become strung out and scattered over the land as more and more of them became too tired to continue and stopped running in an effort to catch up with their knights. They saw the desperate flight of the panic-stricken knights coming back towards them. So they turned and ran as well. Many threw down their weapons as they scattered in all directions.

My men, at least most of them, did as I had trained them and threaded their way through the barons' fleeing foot soldiers and unhorsed knights without getting too close to them. Riding safely through fleeing foot soldiers is important because a man on foot with a sword or spear can bring down a horseman as he rides past. A few of my men forgot what they had been learnt and went down themselves when they rode too near to a man on foot while they were chasing after a fleeing horseman. It was inevitable. Shite happens.

In the end, less than forty of my totally exhausted horse archers made it all the way back to the barons' now-destroyed encampment to join up with George and Richard and what was left of their outriders. Behind us we had left miles and miles of dead and wounded men and horses, including a good number of our own.

My men were greatly chuffed and pleased and full of themselves despite being so stiff and tired they could barely stay in the saddle. Of course they were; they were alive and there were valuable weapons and armour scattered about everywhere that would provide each of us with a good deal of prize money.

It was no wonder the horse archers were so pleased with themselves; many of the young ones, including Richard, my apprentice sergeant, had never before had coins to spend and most of my veterans had none in their pouches because they tended to spend their annual coins and prize monies as quickly as they got them.

My own dear wife would be most pleased with my share of the prize money. I may have to take her to London to spend the coins she does not squirrel away in the little pouch I am not supposed to know about.

Chapter Twenty-one

No rest for the winners.

All the rest of that long summer day was spent searching the battlefield for our survivors and our dead, and gathering up the weapons, armour, and useful clothes of the barons' dead and wounded men. And that included pulling or cutting out the arrows sticking in them. We hitched our horses to abandoned carts and retraced our steps to pick them up. Along the way, as you might imagine we met some of the barons' men who tried to surrender and, of course, many of their wounded.

We took the weapons of the men who wanted to surrender and left them alive with orders to take care of their own wounded. We certainly could not take care of them ourselves; we had enough problems taking care our own wounded, and only a limited supply of the flower paste that stops the pain of a wound. We also ignored the small groups of the barons' men who had ridden or run off into the nearby forest to hide, or left the battlefield and began to ride or walk for home.

That night we camped near the barons' devastated encampment. We lit cooking fires, fed flower paste and water to our wounded men, and ate our fill of burnt strips of horse meat and raw liver. We could hear the murmur of talking in the barons' camp and every so often when the wind blew towards us we could hear cries and moans as wounded men called for help or tried to crawl away.

It was a fine moonlit night and I slept soundly until it was my turn to stand watch. Then, for some reason, the cries of agony and calls for help coming from the barons' camp began to distress me. In the morning there were mostly dead men and horses in the barons' camp and great flocks of birds eating on them.

Many of the barons' men who had been wounded had crawled away in the night. Only a few able-bodied men could be seen moving about. Some were probably the friends and family members of the dead and wounded who had crept back in the night to assist them; others had returned in an effort to scavenge whatever of value might have been left in the camp.

Their scavenging was mostly futile, of course, because we had already removed everything of value to our own camp and given mercies to the horses and men who had no hope. Some of the would-be scavengers at the camp and on the battlefield were killed, but most were sent off with fleas in their ears and a warning that they had be shown no mercy if we ever saw them again.

****** *Richard*

The morning after the battle, after we had broken our fast before dawn with burnt strips of horse meat, Lieutenant Raymond announced that George and I were to ride to Launceston with him to report on what has happened and get more flower paste to sooth our wounded. The rest of the men were to stay in camp to protect the loot we had gathered and tend to our wounded.

George and I rode together with Raymond and the three of us shared our recent experiences. It took less than three hours for the comfortable ambling gait of our horses to get us to the Launceston ford, the gateway to Cornwall. As we approached it, we saw a party of a dozen or so mounted archers splash their way across the river and start down the road towards us.

After a few tense moments, we greeted each other with great enthusiasm. Reports of a big battle and the routing of the barons' army had reached Cornwall yesterday afternoon and they had been sent by Captain William to try to discover what they could about the battle and its aftermath, the very things we were coming

to report. They turned around and rode back with us.
 We did not stop to talk.

Only after our horses splashed across the river
could we see the prepared battle lines of the company's
army. We saw them as we came up on to the river bank
on the Cornwall side after we crossed the ford. The lines
were there with their sharpened stakes, trip holes, and
caltrops, but many of the men were not—they were a
couple of miles away practicing their archery and
marching together on the same foot to the beat of a
drum.

****** *William*

My lieutenants and I, and particularly Thomas, had
been extremely worried about George and the
company's horse archers based at Okehampton ever
since late yesterday afternoon. That was when the
riders we had sent into Devon to see what was
happening had come hurrying back to report that a big
battle with heavy fighting and many dead and wounded
men seemed to underway between the barons' army
marching on Cornwall and another army which seemed
to have a lot of mounted archers.

George and all of our properly gaited horses and
available riders had already been sent to reinforce
Raymond's horse archers based at Okehampton. They

were the only mounted archers we knew about and we assumed they had either sallied out against the barons, or had left the castle before the siege started in order to harry them.

Until we saw Raymond and George, we did not know what had befallen Raymond's horse archers and we were greatly worried because of the reports we had received that the battle had resulted in many dead and wounded men. So we had scraped together a mounted scouting party composed of my personal couriers and other volunteers and sent them into Devon this morning to see what they could find out.

I was stunned and Thomas's face turned white when we heard our lookouts shout that our party of scouts was returning. It was much too soon and we instantly feared the worst. Did they turn back because they met the barons' victorious army on the road to Cornwall? I was about to summon our archers to man their fighting positions when I saw our scouting party splash its way over the ford—and realized they were not alone.

"My God, look Thomas; it is George and Raymond."

Thomas and I literally ran to meet them, and so did many others.

"What happened?" I shouted with great relief in my voice as my son dismounted and I gave him a big fatherly hug. "Are you all right? We heard there was a battle and many fell. Is it true?"

I was so relieved to see him that I could barely contain myself.

A very pleased and smiling Raymond answered, as he should being as he held the highest rank.

"Aye Captain, we had a great battle. We won it, and the barons and their men are defeated and running. It is finished; the war is over. We have ridden in to report and get another chest of flower paste for our wounded."

"Finished? You defeated the barons' army and it ran? How can that be?"

It was hard to believe. I was truly astonished and so was everyone else.

******

It took a while for my lieutenants and me to fully understand what had occurred because each of the men had a fine tale to tell and was anxious to tell it. By the time they finished, a great circle of men had gathered around them and what each of the three men said was repeated by those who were able to hear them to those who were standing further away and could not. There was much cheering and clapping of hands as each man told his tale.

I decided right then and there that I would go to the battlefield to see for myself and take some men to help with the wounded and bring the captured weapons and such back to Cornwall. And then, at Thomas's suggestion that "it would be good thing for everyone to be learnt what a few good men could do with proper training and the latest weapons," I decided that we would all march there so everyone could see what happened and be inspired by it. *Little did I know that this would turn out to be an unfortunate mistake.*

******

My lieutenants and I left for the battlefield almost immediately with six full ship's companies marching behind us to the beat of their rowing drums. The rest would assemble and follow within the hour. I was still so worried about the barons' army, particularly since I was told that the Earl of Devon's body had not been found, that I had each ship's company march with its auxiliaries and its horse carts filled with its land fighting weapons and supplies. *I still could not grasp the size or extent of the victory.*

We could smell the death in the barons' final encampment and see the circling birds long before we reached it late in the morning. It was not until I finally saw the barons' camp that I began to realize just how great the victory was that George and Richard and their handful of outriders had won here. It was right then and there that I decided that every man who fought in the battle should be rewarded with another stripe except, of course, Raymond, because there was no higher rank possible except captain and I already held it. He would get a reward of two hundred silver coins and be a very rich man for the rest of his life.

One of the companies of foot archers was ordered to stay at the barons' camp to salvage the abandoned carts and wains. They were also to provide assistance or mercies to the remaining enemy wounded as might be required, many of whom had already been removed by their friends and relatives to a more comfortable site immediately upwind of the camp.

"Feed them and let them go," I ordered, somewhat unnecessarily, since I could see that their friends and relatives had scavenged the makings of bread from the destroyed supplies and were burning meat from the barons' dead horses and oxen. *What I was really saying to the archers, of course, was that the war was over and those of our enemies who survived should be left alone to walk home.*

The rest of the companies were ordered to spread out in a great line and walk close together over the battlefield beyond the barons' encampment to retrieve any missing weapons and enemy wounded. My lieutenants and I led them. It took all the rest of the day because Raymond's "wounded bird" had led the barons' riders such a great distance from their camp and so many had fallen.

That night we camped near the spot where Raymond turned around and began his counterattack. It was a pleasant night and we spent it sleeping in the open after a splendid meal of fresh flatbread and burnt meat strips cut from the barons' horses that had not yet spoilt. There was much singing and moors dancing.

******

We left an entire company of foot archers to clean up and the wounded bird battle field and marched the rest of the archers to Okehampton the next morning. It took almost all day to get there and my lieutenants and I talked almost constantly as we rode slowly at the front of our marching men. We had many important things to discuss even though my thoughts increasingly turned towards seeing Isabel. First among them was the Earl of Devon and Exeter Castle.

"The Earl was not found among the dead," I said to my lieutenants as we rode together. "Do we dare attack him now that we know he and the other barons came against us with the permission of King John? Or should we be content to hold Okehampton to guard the approaches to Cornwall?"

After much discussion, Thomas convinced us that we should do nothing until we know more about the King's thoughts and intentions. He offered a good idea that I instantly accepted.

"Master Levi might know," Thomas suggested. "Why do not you send a parchment to London and ask him?"

Another question I raised as we rode together had to do with the port of Hastings. I had recognized some of the Hastings men who had tormented us among the barons' dead and wounded. I asked my lieutenants what they thought about our sending a couple of galleys to return their heads to Hastings, and, while they were there, either burn all the boats in the harbour or require the city to pay another ransom for allowing its men to attack us, or both

I was still seething about how the Hasting portsmen tortured and mistreated my men and me when we were wrecked near there and held for ransom. Cutting that bastard portsman's belly open and making the others pay a ransom instead of getting one from us was not near enough; their joining with the barons had reminded me of an earlier pledge I had yet to kept.

"That was another good question for Master Levi." Thomas opined.

******

We were approaching Okehampton on its cart path, and I was thinking how pleasant it might be to see Isabel again, when an exhausted galloper came in from the sergeant who had been left in command of our Restormel garrison. One of our picket galleys at the port of Haarlem had come in with an important parchment addressed to me.

The message on the parchment was alarming to read and changed everything, including my plan to spend a few days at Okehampton—one of the German princes was coming for the relics with both enough coins to buy them and a very large army. The talk in the taverns of Haarlem, where the German prince's armada stopped for food and water, was that he intended to buy them only if he could not seize them or force us to give them up.

"There is trouble coming, lads," I told my lieutenants. "We need to get our men back to Restormel and aboard their galleys as fast as possible."

- End of the Book –

There are more books in *The Company of Archers Saga*.

All of the books in this exciting and action-packed medieval saga are available on Amazon as individual eBooks. Some of them are also available in print and as audio books. Many of them are available in multi-book collections. You can find them by searching for *Martin Archer Stories*.

This book is book ten of the saga and can also be found in a bargain-priced collection containing books 7,

8, 9, and 10 entitled *The Archers' Story: Part II.* The three books after that are collected as *The Archers' Story Part III;* and the four after that are collected in *The Archers' Story: Part IV.* There is also a *Part V* with the next three and a collection entitled Part VI after that.

A chronological list of all the books in the saga, and other books by Martin Archer, can be found below.

Finally, a word from Martin:

"I sincerely hope you enjoyed reading the stories about the hard men of Britain's first great merchant and military company as much as I have enjoyed writing it. If so, I hope you will consider reading the other stories in the saga and leaving a favourable review on Amazon or Google with as many stars as possible in order to encourage other readers.

"And, if you could please spare a moment, I would also very much appreciate your thoughts and suggestions about this saga and its stories from the dawn of Britain's rise as a great economic and military power. Should the stories continue? What do you think? I can be reached at martinarcherV@gmail.com."

Cheers and thank you once again. /S/ Martin Archer

Books in the exciting and action-packed *The Company of Archers* saga:

The Archers

The Archers' Castle

The Archers' Return

The Archers' War

Rescuing the Hostages

Archers and Crusaders

The Archers' Gold

The Missing Treasure

Castling the King

The Sea Warriors

eBooks in Martin Archer's epic *Soldiers and Marines* saga:

Soldiers and Marines

Peace and Conflict

War Breaks Out

War in the East (A fictional tale of America's role in the next great war)

Israel's Next War (A prescient book much hated by Islamic reviewers)

Collections of Martin Archer's books on Amazon

The Archers Stories I - complete books I, II, III, IV, V, and VI

The Archers Stories II - complete books VII, VIII, IX, and X

The Archers Stories III - complete books XI, XII, and XIII

The Archers Stories IV – complete books XIV, XV, XVI, and XVII

The Archers Stories V – complete books XVIII, XIX, and XX

The Archers Stories VI - complete books XXI, XXII, XXIII

The Soldiers and Marines Saga - complete books I, II, and III

Other eBooks you might enjoy:

Cage's Crew by Martin Archer writing as Raymond Casey

America's Next War by Michael Cameron – an adaption of Martin Archer's *War Breaks Out* to set it in the immediate future when Eastern and Western Europe go to war over another wave of Islamic refugees.

Sample pages from the first book in the saga.

.... I decided to leave George with the archers whilst my brother Thomas and I went into the city to try to find the Bishop and collect our pay—four bezant gold coins from Constantinople for each man. And we would get more for every man in the company who had lost his life or balls whilst with Edmund. It was quite a bit for only two years of service, but we had paid dearly for it by so many of us losing our lives.

At least we tried to get in see the Bishop. The guards at the city gate would not let us through the gate even though Thomas was a priest.

One of the guards looked a little bit smarter and greedier than the other two. Thomas motioned him aside and blessed him. I watched as they huddled together for a moment talking in low voices.

Then Thomas waved me over.

"William, this good man cannot leave his post to tell the Bishop we are here. And that is a pity for we only need to see His Eminence for a few minutes to deliver the important message we are bringing him.

"It is a problem we need to solve because it would not be a Christian thing to make someone as important as the good Bishop upset. He is sure to be unhappy if he has to walk all this way just to have a word with us."

"Ah. I understand. The guard wants a bribe to let us in.

"Let us in and you and the others can come with us when we sail away from here," I said.

"Forget it, English. I have a wife and family here. I am not going anywhere."

It was time to take another tack. I reached into my almost empty purse and pulled out two small copper coins—enough for a night of drinking if the wine was bad enough. I pressed them into his grimy hand.

"We only need a few minutes to deliver a message. We will be out and gone before anyone knows."

The guard looked at the coins and then again at us, sizing us up was what he was doing. And he did not like what he saw. We looked like what we were, poor and bedraggled.

"One more copper. There are three of us on duty and no one is supposed to enter. But we will take a chance, since it is for the Bishop and our sergeant is not here."

I agreed with a sigh and dug out another copper.

"We will not be long and the Bishop will appreciate it." *No, he will not.*

Thomas waved the wooden cross he wore around his neck to bless the guard as he put our coppers in his purse, and then he waved it at the other two for good measure.

******

Thomas and I had to shoulder our way through the crowded streets and push people away as we walked towards the church. Beggars and desperate women and young boys began pulling on our clothes and crying out to us. In the distance black smoke was rising from somewhere in the city, probably from looters torching somebody's house or shop.

The doors to the front of the church were barred. Through the cracks in the wooden doors we could see the big wooden bar holding them shut.

"Come on. There must be a side door for the priests to use. There always is."

We walked around to the side of the church and there it was. I began banging on the door. After a while, a muffled voice on the other side told us to go away.

"Go away. The church is not open."

"We have come from Lord Edmund to bring a message to the Bishop of Damascus. Let us in."

We could hear something being moved and then an eye appeared at the peep hole in the door. A few seconds later, the door swung open and we hurried in.

The light inside the room was dim because the windows were shuttered.

Our greeter was a slender fellow with alert eyes who could not have been much more than an inch or two over five feet tall. He studied us intently as he bowed us in and then quickly shut and barred the door behind us. He seemed quite anxious.

"We have come from the Bekka Valley to see the Bishop," I said in the bastardised French dialect some call crusader French and others are now calling English. And then Thomas repeated my words in Latin. *Which, of course, is what I should have done in the first place?*

"I shall tell His Eminence that you are here and ask if he will receive you," the man replied in Latin. "I am Yoram, the Bishop's scrivener; may I tell him who you are and why you are here?"

"I am William, the captain of what is left of a company of English archers, and this is Father Thomas, our priest. We are here to collect our pay for helping to defend Lord Edmund's fief these past two years."

"I shall inform His Eminence of your arrival. Please wait here." *The Bishop' scrivener had a strange accent; I wondered where he came from?*

Some minutes passed before the anxious little man returned. Whilst he was gone we looked around the room inside the door. It was quite luxurious with a floor of stones instead of the mud floors one usually finds in churches.

It was also quite dark. The windows were covered with heavy wooden shutters and sealed shut with heavy wooden bars; the light in the room, such as it was, came from cracks in the shutters and smaller windows high on the walls above the shuttered windows. There was a somewhat tattered tribal carpet on the floor.

The anxious little man returned and gave us a most courteous nod and bow.

"His Grace will see you now. Please follow me."

The Bishop's clerk led us into a narrow, dimly lit passage with stone walls and a low ceiling. He went first and then Thomas and then me. We had taken but a few steps when he turned back toward us and in an intense low voice issued a terse warning.

"Protect yourselves. The Bishop does not want to pay you. You are in mortal danger."

The little man nodded in silent agreement when I held up my hand. Thomas and I needed to take a moment to get ourselves ready.

His eyes widened, and he watched closely as we prepared. Then, when I gave a nod to let him know we were ready, he rewarded us with a tight smile and another nod of agreement—and began walking again with a particularly determined look on his face.

A few seconds later we turned another corner and came to an open wooden door. It opened into a large room with beamed ceilings more than six feet high and stone walls begrimed by centuries of smoke. I knew the height because I could stand upright after I bent my head to get through the entrance door.

A portly, middle-aged man in a bishop's robes was sitting behind a table covered with parchments. There was a bearded and rather formidable-looking guard with a sword in a wooden scabbard standing in front of the table on our side of it. There was also a closed chest on the table, a pile of parchments, and a jumble of tools and chests in the corner covered by another old tribal rug. A broken chair was pushed up against the wall.

The Bishop smiled to show us his bad teeth, and beckoned us in. We could see him clearly despite the dim light coming in from five or six small window openings near the ceiling of the room.

After a moment, the bishop stood up and extended his hand over the table so we could kiss his ring. First Thomas and then I approached and half kneeled to kiss it. Then I stepped back and towards the guard to make room for Thomas so he could re-approach the table and stand next to me as the Bishop re-seated himself.

"What is it you want to see me about?" the Bishop asked in Latin.

He said it with a sincere smile and leaned forward expectantly.

"I am William, captain of the late Lord Edmund's company of English archers, and this is Father Thomas, our priest and confessor." *And my older brother, though I did not think it wise to mention it at that moment.*

"How can that be? Another man was commanding the archers when I visited Lord Edmund earlier this year, and we made our arrangements."

"He is dead. He took an arrow in the arm and it turned purple and rotted until he died. Another took his place and now he is dead also. Now I am the captain of the company."

The Bishop crossed himself and mumbled a brief prayer under his breath. Then he looked at me expectantly and listened intently.

"We have come to get the coins Lord Edmund gave to you to hold for us so we would be paid if he fell. We looked for you before we left the valley, but Beaufort Castle was about to fall and you had already gone. So we have come here to collect our pay."

"Of course. Of course. I have it right here in the chest.

"Aran," he said, nodding to the burly soldier standing next to me, "tells me there are eighteen of you. Is that correct?" *And how would he be knowing that?*

"Yes, Eminence, that is correct."

"Well then, four gold Constantinople coins for each man totals seventy-two; and you shall have them here and now."

"No, Eminence, that is not correct."

I reached inside my jerkin and pulled out the company's copy of the contract with Lord Edmund, laid the parchment on the desk in front of him, and turned it around so he could read the words in Latin that had been scribed on it and see Edmund's mark.

As I placed the contract on the table, I tapped it with my finger and casually stepped further to the side, and even closer to his swordsman. I did it so Thomas could once again step into my place in front of the Bishop and nod his agreement, confirming it was indeed in our contract.

"Our contract calls for four gold bezant coins from Constantinople for each of seventy-nine men, and six more coins to the company for each man who was killed or lost both of his eyes or his bollocks. It sums to one thousand and twenty-six bezants in all—and I know you have our money because I was present when Lord Edmund gave you many more coins and you agreed to pay them to us. We are here to collect our coins."

"Oh yes. So you are. So you are. Of course. Well, you shall certainly get what is due you. God wills it."

I sensed the swordsman stiffen as the Bishop said the words and opened the lid of the chest. The Bishop reached in with both hands and took a big handful of bezants in his left hand and placed them on the table.

He spread the gold coins out on the table and motioned Thomas forward to help him count as he reached back in to fetch another handful. I stepped further to the left and even closer to the guard so Thomas would have plenty of room to step forward to help the Bishop count.

Everything happened at once when Thomas leaned forward to start counting the coins. The Bishop reached again into his money chest as if to get another handful. This time he came out with a dagger—and lunged across the coins on the table to drive it into Thomas's chest with a grunt of satisfaction.

The swordsman next to me simultaneously began pulling his sword from its wooden scabbard. It had all been prearranged. .....

18344709R00163